STO

FRIENDS
OF ACPL

W9-BBG-944

Let 'em Roll

Let 'em Roll

written and illustrated by

CHARLES MICHAEL DAUGHERTY

1950

THE VIKING PRESS : NEW YORK

COPYRIGHT 1950 BY CHARLES MICHAEL DAUGHERTY

FIRST PUBLISHED BY THE VIKING PRESS IN APRIL 1950

PUBLISHED ON THE SAME DAY IN THE DOMINION OF CANADA

BY THE MACMILLAN COMPANY OF CANADA LIMITED

PRINTED IN THE UNITED STATES OF AMERICA
BY THE VAIL-BALLOU PRESS, INC.

To My Mother and Father

CO. SCHOOLS

C471094

Contents

Let 'em Roll

I. The Sooner the Better

"Maybe you'd better let me drive for a while, Josh," said Mr. Beacon. His quiet voice held an unmistakable note of warning.

"Aw shucks, Dad. I've only been driving for an hour."

"All right then, but the next time you go over fifty we change places."

"Okay," sighed Joshua, easing the pressure of his foot on the accelerator. He hadn't meant to go quite so fast. The car was only a few months old. It had hardly been broken in, and he knew better than to push it past fifty. But it hummed along so smoothly that no matter what he did it

11

seemed to float across the countryside without so much as touching the ground. If it weren't for the tattling speedometer on the dashboard nobody would even know that he was speeding.

Fast or slow, however, Joshua was obviously a young man in a hurry. He managed to honor his father's admonition by maintaining a steady forty-nine and a half miles per hour—but not for long.

It was the voice of his mother that brought attention to his next violation of the speed limit. "Joshua," she asked with a disarming show of innocence, "do you know what month this is?"

"Sure, Mother. It's June. Why?"

"I was just wondering. We have July and August in which to drive from New York to California and back. At the rate you're taking us we'll only need about two weeks for the whole trip. What are you going to do with all the leftover time?"

"Golly, Mother, you know what I'm going to do with it. I want to learn all I can about the movies. If we get out there in time Uncle Tex says—" he checked himself with a rueful grin. His father was silently thumbing him to the side of the road with the relentless gesture of a motorcycle cop. There was nothing to do but stop, surrender the wheel, and withdraw to the back of the car.

With Mr. Beacon driving, the family rode on in silence. In the back, since his mother had moved to the front, Joshua had the whole wide seat to himself. By leaning his head back and stretching his legs diagonally across the tops of the suitcases which were stacked on the floor, he was able to settle down into an almost horizontal position. This, he consoled himself, was solid comfort.

It was midafternoon. Ahead and all around, the Kansas landscape lay as flat as a sea beneath the vast gray sky. The scene was big and empty. The scattered farm buildings that slipped past seemed very lonely. It felt good to be in a comfortable automobile smoothly gobbling up the miles. The country might be flat and the weather gray, but tomorrow and tomorrow could be counted on to bring new landscapes and even different climates. It was impossible to remain downcast for long under the circumstances. Joshua's spirits, briefly dampened by disgrace at the wheel, were soon soaring. The chromium radiator cap steadily pointed the way.

Ahead was California and the bright prospect of nearly two whole vacation months. Last winter, when the family first began to talk about a trip west, Joshua had taken prompt action to revive a sporadic correspondence with his uncle in Hollywood. An exchange of brief but spirited letters revealed an enthusiasm for moving pictures that seemed to have grown as ardent in the schoolboy as it was in the rising young director.

Tex Beacon was the star by which Joshua had steered for almost as long as he could remember. He had never seen a great deal of him, but the few times that his uncle had been east to visit were memorable occasions. The thing about Tex, Joshua maintained, was that he made you feel like an equal—as though he were a boy as well as a man, and you were a man as well as a boy.

Under the influence of such a hero Joshua naturally intended to be a moving-picture director himself some day. Never had he wavered before an impulse to follow the career of detective, fireman, ball player, or congressman. The three elapsed years of his high school career had been undistinguished except for a few triumphant hours on the football field—and The Movie.

The Movie was an achievement of which he felt justifiably proud. It had begun as an idea even before he entered high school: why not make a class history on film? Then Tex had given him a 16 mm. camera as a birthday present and the idea became a practical possibility. He had begun his freshman year by filming as much as possible of the first day of school. In the beginning they had laughed at him for his persistent picture-taking, but he kept at it, using the half-dozen rolls of color film that had come with the camera. He had taken sequences of football practice, of the rally before the big game, of the band, of the teachers, and of nearly everyone in the class.

One morning he had run the pictures off at assembly and at the same time explained his idea in front of the entire school. From then on it had been an official class project. As the footage on class activities and personalities had accumulated, general interest and support had grown. The highlights of freshman, sophomore, and junior years had

been recorded by his camera. Next spring he and his helpers would edit their four years of film and have not only a complete class history in colored movies but a real documentary picture of school life.

During that first year The Movie had kept Joshua and his uncle in close contact by mail. In addition to an expert's answers to his problems, Joshua got advice and encouragement, which inspired him to develop his own approach to picture making. But as he obtained increasingly successful results and at the same time became further involved in school activities, he found less and less time for writing letters. The correspondence dwindled, but not the friendship. And while the boy was growing, so was his uncle's reputation. Pictures like *The Wild, Wild West* and *Overland Trails* were talked about and written about and highly praised with such complimentary words as "original," "inspiring," and "stirring."

Now, after years devoted to reading and thinking movies, Joshua's fondest dream was about to materialize. Ahead was the movie-making capital of the world. And in his pocket he carried the latest word from Tex, received just before they left home. It was hurried but cordial. To Joshua in his eagerness it even seemed urgent.

"Very busy at the moment," the director had written. "Am in the midst of shooting a picture that is scheduled to be made in forty days. I'm going on location but will certainly be home by the time you arrive. And by the way, old boy, if you get here in time, maybe you can get into a few scenes as an extra. Anyway, I imagine you'll want to see as much of everything as possible. So come on—the sooner the better."

The sooner the better. But his mother and father were inclined to overlook any necessity for speed. Not that they could be called unsympathetic. The opportunity for Joshua to visit a moving-picture studio had been one of the prime factors in deciding the trip. But now that they were on their way they were determined to see as much of the country as possible while they were about it. With complete disregard for the fact that an entire picture might be filmed in forty days, they insisted that what they considered a reasonable pace would be sufficient to get them to their destination in time enough to satisfy everybody. Dad, who sometimes seemed to regard curiosity as the highest of human virtues, was morbidly interested in historic sites, and it appeared that there were nearly as many of them along the road as there were telephone poles.

Only this morning he had wasted an entire half-day in Independence, Missouri, because, he explained, a hundred years ago it used to be the jumping-off place for the old wagon caravans to the West. Today it looked much like any other small, busy, up-to-date Midwestern city, but he had to look up the old log courthouse, and the place where until recently a frontier blacksmith shop had stood, and to describe enthusiastically how this very site had once been jammed with the heavy traffic of history's greatest migration, preparing for the long journey into the wilderness. And finally he had spent an hour talking with an ancient character who went on and on about how his grandfather had been a teamster on the Santa Fe Trail.

The worst of the sight-seeing was that one thing always led to another. As a result of the delay in Independence, nothing would do but that they themselves must continue on their way via the old wagon route to Santa Fe. So instead of having left Kansas City by the main highway to the Southwest, they were heading over a back road for a place called Council Grove.

From Joshua's point of view it was an unfortunate change in plan. At times like this, when the going seemed much too slow, he liked to pore over the road map for comfort. He could sometimes find satisfaction in reviewing the distance already put behind and mentally speeding over the roads ahead. He got the map out now and spread it on the seat beside him. Here was Kansas, right in the middle of the United States. After a close scrutiny he located Council Grove. It was a tiny place, situated on the Neosho River, in the southern part of the state. He was able to find some consolation in the fact that when they got there they could at least call their journey to the coast half done. He also found that the total distance to California wasn't noticeably any farther by this route than it would be the regular way. But how much sight-seeing time was Council Grove going to take? What was it that could make this one-horse town worth going out of the way to see? As he speculated about the delay that now confronted them, he became increasingly uneasy until he could no longer refrain from attempting to sound out his father on the matter.

"Dad," he ventured, trying to phrase his question tactfully enough to disguise its real purpose, "why did they go to Council Grove?"

"Who, Josh?"

"Those wagon trains."

"Oh, the wagon trains. Well, you'll be able to see for yourself when we get there. It was just a point on the way to Santa Fe, of course, but it was an important one."

This wasn't quite the way he had meant the conversation to go. As a matter of fact he hadn't gotten one going at all, for his father lapsed back into silence, concentrating on the road ahead and apparently content to wait for Council Grove to explain itself.

THE SOONER THE BETTER 19

After a short silence Joshua cleared his throat in preparation for another try. "Who," he inquired this time, "was going to Santa Fe a hundred years ago, and why?" It seemed like a stupid question in view of the fact that everyone out here apparently knew all about it, but he had never been much good at history, and anyway he couldn't remember that the Santa Fe Trail had ever come up in school.

To his surprise, however, his father seemed to accept this as a perfectly legitimate question. "Quite a lot of people were going to Santa Fe a hundred years ago," he answered after a moment's thought, "and most of them were going for a simple enough reason—to make money. In those days the country called New Mexico was not part of the United States. Like California, it was a province of Mexico. Santa Fe was its capital. Up until 1821, when Mexico gained her independence from Spain, the people of Santa Fe depended on Spanish merchants and officials for their commerce with the outside world. These men, naturally enough, were jealous of foreign trade competition. They wanted all the provincial business for themselves. But after Mexico became an independent republic, trade between New Mexico and the States began to pick up. After all, it was no harder for caravans to cross these plains that we're crossing now than it was to make the long journey to Chihuahua in old Mexico. And Mexicans had a hankering for Yankee notions. They could pay for them with silver and gold and mules. So if an American had a few dollars to invest and was willing to take the risk, the chances were he could make a good profit by freighting a wagonload of shawls and looking glasses, hardware and cotton goods, down the trail in the annual spring caravan to Santa Fe."

"Was there actually a road in those days?" asked Joshua.

"Well, no, nothing like the one we're on now. The trail

was really people and animals and wagons, taking the most likely way across the plains and deserts. It followed several routes. But from the Missouri frontier towns they almost always went to Council Grove. At ox pace it took around ten days to cover the hundred and fifty miles that we're doing in a few hours this afternoon. The entire journey to Santa Fe, with a little luck, took five or six weeks."

A soft whistle from the back seat indicated that Joshua was at last impressed. His mother chuckled. "There you are," she said cheerily. "*We* aren't doing so badly after all."

"Ten days," said Joshua. "Wow!" Reflectively he lay back in his seat to watch the flow of passing landscape with renewed interest. The fever of urgency that had burned so hotly all day began to ease. Now and then a jack rabbit bounced across the road like a hard-driven, high-bouncing ball. He picked up the map again and studied it. Hollywood didn't look quite so far away as it had only a few minutes before.

II. The Wagons Roll

To Joshua's unenthusiastic eye Council Grove was a one-horse town. But as a matter of fact the commercial center, consisting principally of several blocks of one- to three-story buildings facing each other across a wide main street, displayed a fair share of the standardized, up-to-date features which distinguish nearly all American towns no matter how small or isolated they may be. In the early sunlight of a sparkling summer morning not a single horse was in evidence, although numerous automobiles were

parked head-in along the curbs; here a delivery truck stood with motor idling before a familiar chain grocery store, and there a ponderous trailer turned in at a service station to deliver gasoline.

Anyone not too impatient to take a good look around could recognize a self-respecting community which, though small, prided itself both on being up-to-date and having a past. The previous evening, entering the town at dusk, Mr. Beacon, who was seldom too impatient to look around, had lost no time in identifying the little park and the statue of the pioneer woman with a baby in her arms which marked the old camp site by the river. After dinner, while Joshua and his mother went to a movie, he had visited the public library to find out what he could about the place. Council Grove, he learned, was called the most historic Kansas town on the Santa Fe Trail. The name referred to the stand of big trees bordering the Neosho River. There a treaty had once been made with the Indians. It was the last timber crossing to Santa Fe, which meant that before a building ever stood on this site travelers had made a custom of camping to fill their water casks, cut timber for repairs along the treeless trail, and organize their caravans for the long journey which lay ahead.

In the morning, cruising slowly down Main Street in order to look around by daylight, Mr. Beacon was able to point out the places of interest as though he had been here before. Joshua, as he half listened, couldn't help wondering just how many of them there were going to be. They had gotten up and off to an early start today. Hopes were

high for a good day's run if only they didn't have to devote too much time to the most historic town on the Santa Fe Trail.

They took another look at the river and at the little park presided over by the statue of the pioneer woman and her child. Then, after turning up an abrupt hill, they climbed for a minute to discover a wide view of the surrounding countryside. To the west an immense plain stretched flat and empty until it met the edges of the sky. In silent surprise they stopped to gaze over the panorama they had so unexpectedly come upon.

"There," Mr. Beacon finally said. "There is the Great American Desert."

"Is that what a desert looks like?" asked Joshua in a disappointed tone. "I thought deserts were nothing but sand."

"Not always," said his father. "Desert—comes from deserted. It means any great area of barren land. The Great Plains and the Rocky Mountains used to be considered a good-for-nothing wilderness where civilized people would never be able to live. On the old maps the whole unexplored area was labeled the Great American Desert. When you look out there it's not hard to understand how they made such a mistake."

"Little Council Grove," observed Mrs. Beacon, "must have been like an oasis."

"That's just what it was. After a caravan left here it was up against Indians, the danger of water shortage, and all the hazards of a long journey through a sun-parched wilderness. And yet people by the thousands traveled this trail—not only for profit, but for adventure and sport, and even for the sake of health."

"It makes you think," said Mrs. Beacon. "History isn't just a lot of dates. It's the life stories of all the people who ever lived, and are living today."

"Golly, I guess that's right," said Joshua in reluctant agreement.

"Of course it's right," said his mother. "It's the most exciting story in the world."

As they were talking, Mr. Beacon had started the car. He drove down from the hilltop, turned right on Main Street, and headed out of town toward the open expanse they had just been overlooking. "After they left the river," he said, "they kept to whatever ridges or high ground there might be, in order to have a good view in all directions and watch out for Indians. A man told me last night that there are a couple of places near here where you can still see the ruts of the wagon wheels in the ground."

For an apprehensive minute Joshua wondered if they were now going to look for wagon ruts. Although the remarks just made in regard to history had given him something to think about, it still seemed to him that a rut in the ground was after all nothing but—well, a rut in the ground.

To his relief, however, it soon became apparent that they were actually leaving Council Grove behind them. The sight-seeing had not taken long after all. Joshua was

secretly a little ashamed of himself for having worried so
much over this imaginary obstacle.

The morning was still fresh. Dew glistened on the grass,
and golden prairie flowers glowed against the blue sky. He
unfolded the map across his knees to learn what kind of
roads lay ahead today. Except for a stretch of fifteen or
twenty miles that appeared to be unpaved, it looked like
smooth rolling. At least there weren't going to be any towns
either big enough or historic enough to make much difference for a little while.

The miles and hours passed easily. In the afternoon
Joshua was reinstated as alternate driver. It felt good to
change position and have something to do. He was determined that this time he would keep possession of the
wheel for an honorable period.

Almost as soon as he began driving he came on a stretch
of road under repair. He had no choice but to drive slowly.
When the good surface resumed he kept his speed down
by thinking of the tedious pace of the wagon caravans
they had been talking so much about. He even tried driving at five miles an hour for half a mile in order to get an

idea of what it was like. It seemed like standing still, and yet it was faster than a team of oxen could haul a loaded wagon. When he climbed back to forty-five again he was content to hold it there.

He drove successfully for half the afternoon before trading places again with his father. Then he was satisfied to get in back and rest. He pulled a blanket over his shoulders and soon was nestling down among the baggage in a luxurious snooze.

He didn't know how long he dozed, but the next thing he was aware of was the stopping of the car and sounds of his parents getting out. For a minute he heard their voices but was too drowsy to open his eyes. "This is a good enough place," his father was saying. "We can walk up that rise and stretch our legs and get a little of the feel of the lone prairie."

"Josh is fast asleep." His mother's voice came from outside the car. "We might as well leave him in peace."

"Let him sleep if he wants to. We'll be right back."

He could hear them moving away. Then he briefly napped again. A few minutes later he awoke suddenly, opened his eyes, and wondered where he could be. The quiet car parked beside a deserted road in the middle of an empty prairie made him feel that he might be still asleep, dreaming a fantastic nightmare in which he was the only person left in the world. Not a moving thing was in sight. He remembered, then, why the car stood silently by the deserted road. His mother and father had stopped to take a little walk. Yawning and stretching, he climbed out to loosen his cramped joints and breathe the sweet spring air.

There, about a hundred yards or so from where he stood, was a rise of ground which he assumed to be the one he had heard his parents mention. If he walked to the top of it he might be able to see them.

He waded into the grass, but when he reached what seemed to be the highest elevation he realized that, although he could see the horizon all the way around, the ground was undulating. A moving figure a little way off could be visible against the sky one minute and hidden in a depression the next.

He strolled along the crest of the rise, stretching his legs and expecting to catch sight of his mother and father at any minute. It felt good to move about after having been in the car all day. Soon he had covered more distance than he realized. When he again stopped to look around he found that he was now on the far side of the rise and could see neither the road nor the car. He turned around and strolled leisurely back in the direction from which he had come until he reached the road. The car was nowhere in sight.

With a sinking feeling under his belt he realized that he had sleepily walked off without looking to see if the keys had been taken out of the ignition switch or the doors locked. Yet it hardly seemed probable that anybody could have stolen the car when there was absolutely no one within range of sight or sound. Who, he puzzled, but his parents could have taken it? And, for that matter, how could they have done so when he had been able to find no sign of them in the vicinity?

He stood helplessly by the road, lost and mystified, try- ing to think. It had happened while he was taking his stroll. Perhaps he had missed them while he was on the other side of the ridge. But even if they had come back to the car while he was gone they wouldn't deliberately drive off without him. No, of course not *deliberately*. But they could have left him by mistake. When they had gone for their walk he was asleep with a blanket pulled over him. He had got out and tossed the blanket aside on the luggage-cluttered seat. It was possible that they had re- turned to the car absorbed in conversation and started off without noticing that he was no longer there. It was the kind of absent-minded thing they were quite capable of doing when they got talking.

Yes, he decided, this could be the only solution. He felt easier for having found one. Now there was nothing to do but stick by the road and keep his eyes open until they discovered his absence and came back for him. Alarm gave way to irritation as he realized the further delay that this silly mishap was going to cause. They had been making good time today. Now a large part of what was gained would be lost, and he could blame nobody but himself.

The road, stretching straight across the open prairie, was visible for miles ahead. Too uneasy to stand idle for

long, he soon began to walk in the direction from which, at any moment, he expected he might see the familiar family automobile returning.

There was hardly any traffic. A truck rattled by and slowed to offer him a ride. He was tempted to take it, but he realized that unless he stayed out in plain sight his parents might miss him completely. He had to say "No, thank you." The driver gave him a puzzled look as he drove away.

He kept walking. After about fifteen minutes he came to the beginning of the unpaved road which he had noticed on the map that morning. He felt small and unimportant in such a boundless landscape. There was so much space all around that footsteps seemed futile against it. Yet when he looked over his shoulder he could see behind him a slowly growing chunk of distance already covered.

He found himself thinking of the pioneer travelers, pursuing their paths over this very ground. Alone and afoot, he could believe in them more easily. He was moving at their pace. He could almost imagine what it must have been like to walk across the vast face of the wilderness.

As he hiked and dreamed along the lonely way, it was not, however, a shiny blue automobile that eventually caught his attention. It was something slow and lumbering. At first he didn't know what it could be. It wasn't even on the road, but seemed to rise out of the ground a few hundred yards to the right. It looked like a wagon drawn by oxen. Sunlight gleamed on a ribbed white top. Joshua rubbed his eyes in astonishment. As he did so, another wagon appeared behind the first, and then another. It was —no, it couldn't be. But it unmistakably was a caravan of covered wagons.

"Now I know I'm dreaming," he exclaimed aloud. But even though he had begun to move, like a sleepwalker, from the road toward the apparition on which his gaze was fastened, he was sure of nothing of the sort. On the contrary, he knew that he was as wide awake as he had ever been. He was seeing things. Maybe it was one of those mirages that people see on the desert when they are suffering from thirst. Only he wasn't thirsty in the least—and besides, nobody ever saw a mirage of something that had not existed for a hundred years.

The wagons were moving slowly toward him. There were eight of them in all, accompanied by a number of figures on horseback and a few on foot. When they were close enough for him to make out the faces of bearded men beneath broad-brimmed hats, he began to wonder uneasily

if they could see him. For several seconds he stood still, un-
decided whether or not he should fall to the ground and
hide himself in the grass.

His indecision was abruptly ended by a blood-curdling
yell. From as close to the ground as he could press himself
he was suddenly watching a party of whooping horsemen
fall upon the wagon train. It was an Indian attack.

III. Violent Doings

If Joshua had doubted his eyes, he was compelled to believe his ears. The howls of the Indians, the excited shouts of the teamsters, and the reports of their rifles made a din which was unquestionably genuine.

As he stared in horror at the confused scene he saw it resolve into two rough circles. One was hastily assumed by the wagons, which were formed into a circular barricade with the defenders inside. The other was a whooping merry-go-round of painted and feathered savages who galloped around and around the wagons, brandishing spears and shooting arrows but keeping a respectful distance in spite of their fierce conduct.

C471094

CO. SCHOOLS

It looked, for the moment, as though the initial assault had been parried. A painted warrior hurtled headlong to the ground. Another was thrown as his horse stumbled and went down. At the same time Joshua, hidden in the nearby grass, felt his sudden fright succumbing to reason. He did not yet know what was happening, but, with all the shooting that was going on, he did know that he was too close for comfort. If he could get out of here alive, there would be time enough later to figure out what it was all about. Raising his head as high as the protecting grass would permit, he turned his attention to finding some means of escape.

As he looked around him he noticed, not far to the left, a ragged fringe of grass and a few spots of bald earth that marked some sort of irregularity in the terrain. It might be the rim of a hole, he thought, or at least a furrow in which he could hide himself better. He crawled closer and discovered that he was approaching the edge of a gully, quite wide and deep, which wound from somewhere beyond the battlefield in front of him toward the highway.

Now he could understand why the wagons had seemed to rise up out of the earth. On the flat plain it was impossible to see any abrupt indentation in the ground until it was almost underfoot—or, in Joshua's case, undernose. Only from nearby was the gully visible. If he could worm his way to it and hide in its sunken bed, he would not only feel safer but could probably make a strategic withdrawal to the road.

Wriggling his careful way, he was soon close enough to the edge to make out, through the grass, a glimpse of the opposite bank. A few more feet and he discovered that the gully made a big bend at the place he was approaching. A large part of it was now visible. It looked about thirty or forty feet wide and about eight feet deep. The bottom was a flat earth floor. Near the far side ran the muddy stream which had eroded this winding crevice across the face of the prairie.

The nearer he crawled to the edge, the farther he could see around the sunken bend. With his eyes at the grass tops, he paused before letting himself down into its refuge to peer upstream toward the place where the caravan had made its crossing and the Indians had attacked.

He was startled to see a figure there, just visible at the far curve of the bend. It was a man who was standing with his head thrown back, calmly looking up at the sky. Joshua ducked and pressed the ground with renewed affection. In his ears were the howls and hoofbeats and rifle shots of the Indian fight, but even louder seemed the pounding of his own heart. It hadn't occurred to him that the gully could be just as dangerously peopled as the open ground. Now he miserably realized that any knoll or hollow might hide an Indian. There could be no logical withdrawal from such a fantastic situation. If a ship full of Chinese pirates had appeared on the yellow creek, he could hardly have been more astounded or unnerved.

He lay still for a minute, too numb to think. Then the delayed realization came to him that the man he had just seen was not a Chinese pirate, or an Indian, or, for that matter, anyone of especially remarkable aspect. Slowly he raised his head for another look.

There were now two men standing where the first had been. No, they were certainly not Indians. As far as he could make out they were just two men, dressed in everyday, ordinary clothes. Both of them were looking at the sky. He glanced up to where their attention seemed to be fixed but could see nothing except the blue afternoon sky, bright sun, and a few scattered white clouds. Somewhat reassured by their calm attitudes and normal attire, and compelled by renewed curiosity, he again wriggled to the ledge and raised his head above the grass.

There were even more people beyond the two sky-gazers. He crawled closer. With every yard he moved he could see farther around the bend, until a scene was disclosed that brought him to his knees with a sudden grin of relief and wonder. "So that's it," he said aloud. "I'll be doggoned!"

Several automobiles and light trucks were parked on the floor of the gully. Behind them were a dozen or more figures clustered around a moving-picture camera. From his new position Joshua could now see the whole thing. Although he was almost as astonished as he had been when the caravan first came into sight, he could at least begin to comprehend what was going on.

It was some kind of moving-picture outfit. Why this desolate spot had been chosen was still a mystery. But here they were, and it was obvious that they must have driven up the gully from the road with their cameras and equipment. The position they occupied in the sunken bend hid them from the view of anyone but a nearby observer. The Indian attack was being enacted along the curved, perpendicular embankment. The camera, shooting out through a draw that ran at a tangent to the gully, was taking the scene from a low angle.

Those Indians were actors, and the shots were blank cartridges. Joshua began to chuckle as it dawned on him what a ridiculous thing had happened. He felt a little ashamed of himself, but at the same time he was glad that nobody else need know how completely he had been taken in and just how frightened he had been.

As he knelt there, watching both the camera and the action taking place before it, the sun slid behind a cloud. The Indians abruptly reined in their horses, and the fighting ceased. The galloping, whooping savages of a minute before, and the desperate wagoners, stood quietly studying the sky or adjusting make-up and costumes. Near the camera stood a man with a megaphone to his mouth. Joshua couldn't hear what he was saying but he realized that he must be the director giving the orders.

The cloud responsible for the interruption was only a small one, and as soon as the sun reappeared the actors were back in position, ready to resume their violent doings. The director was poised beside the camera, looking this way and that. Then he raised his megaphone, but instead of turning it on the actors he was throwing his voice directly at Joshua. "Hey! What are you doing in the grass down there?" he was demanding. "Get behind the camera!"

"M-me?" stammered Joshua in a small surprised voice that could be heard only by himself. A number of heads were turned toward him, and he could feel his ears burning. Someone was excitedly motioning him into the gully. Willingly he scrambled over the edge and out of the center of attention. At the same time the sun again dimmed out. To his relief he saw the interest of the director, cameramen, and actors switch back to the troublesome antics of the clouds.

Satisfactorily out of the way and safely ignored as the movie people continued with their own business, Joshua

was seized with an eagerness to get a closer look at them
and their equipment. As long as he didn't intrude on the
camera's field nobody apparently cared what he did. So,
keeping in the gully, close to the stream and as much behind the camera as possible, he approached to within a
short distance of it without attracting further notice.

Cameramen and technicians were too concerned with
the sun overhead, the scene in front of them, and their
respective duties to notice anything else. Some were standing in the attitude of the two men whom Joshua had first
seen in the bend of the gully, looking skyward through
amber filters, while others waited alertly for a chance to
make the most of the precious minutes of remaining sunlight. Seated directly behind the camera and squinting into
the viewer was the director, his megaphone upright on the
ground beside him. Joshua's gaze fastened on him and
followed his every move as though he expected to see him
do some spectacular stunt.

There sat the man who, in his opinion, was making the
picture. Camera and cameramen, technicians and actors,
were indispensable, of course. But they were only the
highly specialized tools with which the director fashioned
the final product.

When the great man got to his feet and stepped away
from the camera, Joshua continued to follow him with ad-
miring eyes. Now that he could plainly see him from the
front for the first time, it occurred to him the the tall thin
figure and shaggy black head had a familiar look. He must

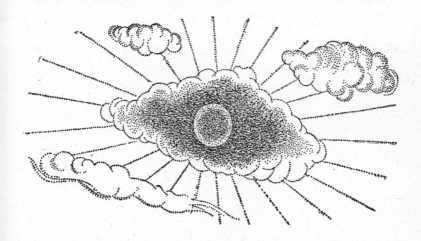

be an actor as well as a director, Joshua thought. He was positive he had seen him before.

He stared harder than ever, trying to place the man. Maybe he had seen him in some picture not so long ago. Then it dawned on him. The director looked like Uncle Tex.

IV. On Location . . . and Mislocation

It hardly seemed possible, yet there he was. There could
be no doubt about it. The director *was* his Uncle Tex.
Joshua impulsively stepped toward him, eager to make
his presence known at once. But at that very instant the

busy man's attention was diverted to a nearby voice which was suddenly raised in sharp remonstrance. Unaware of his nephew almost at his elbow, he turned his back and moved away to find out what the trouble was.

Joshua, although hardly able to contain his excitement, now realized that this was not the right time to interrupt. He would have to wait, but as he stood aside he continued to follow his uncle with his eyes.

He was not the only one watching the director. The attention of a number of those in the vicinity who were waiting at their posts for the sun to shine was attracted by the sound of the angry voice and the incongruous appearance of the two arguers beside whom the director now stood.

The one whose voice was angrily raised had been scurrying around giving orders, and Joshua recognized him as the man who had frantically waved him out of the camera's range only a few minutes previously. He was apparently the assistant director. Short and stocky, he was nattily dressed in a checked jacket and gray flannels. He stood belligerently before his silent adversary like Jack the Giant Killer.

The giant was a gaunt figure in a long, dirty buckskin hunting shirt, the ragged fringes of which reached to his knees. His legs too were clothed in fringed buckskin, and on his feet were a pair of beaded moccasins.

He looked, at first glance, like one of the actors, but closer observation suggested that the gray stubble on the leathery face was not the effect of make-up, and that his clothes were too old and greasy to be a costume.

"What's the matter here?" Tex demanded in a quiet tone.

"This character's been pesterin' me all day long," declared the assistant director. "He keeps sayin' he's gotta talk to the boss, an' I keep tellin' him you're busy."

The old man removed a battered broad-rimmed hat at the director's approach. The towering top of his head was a bald dome. Standing beside him, Tex, who was a tall man himself, came only a little above his shoulder and had to look up into his weathered face.

"Beg pardon, Mister," the giant said. His voice boomed with an astonishingly rich and vigorous clarity. "Beg pardon, but some o' them Comanches yonder is ridin' in mighty fofurraw Mexican saddles. Can't hardly say they're much like old times. An' some o' them is wearin'—"

"Say, who are you anyway?" the director interrupted in surprise.

The old man stopped in mid-sentence with his mouth opened around an unuttered word. It was his turn to show surprise. He shifted his weight from one foot to the other, scratched his bald dome, and after a few seconds recovered himself sufficiently to attempt an answer.

"Me?" he said. "Why I'm the—"

But again he was interrupted, this time by the sun bursting out of the clouds. Immediately the concern of the director and his assistant and of the entire company was

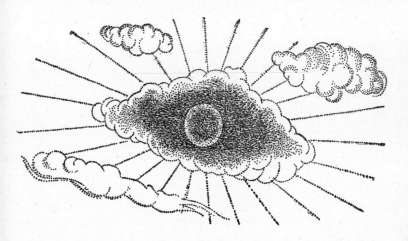

concentrated on taking advantage of the remaining sunlight.

While all hands turned back to their jobs, Joshua continued to scrutinize the old man. Left standing by himself, he looked perplexed, perhaps a little disgusted, and unquestionably forlorn. The boy felt a pang of sympathy and had an impulse to speak to him. But recalling that, for the time being, he was best off completely out of the way, he returned his attention to the renewed activity of the movie makers, and the old man was forgotten.

For ten or fifteen minutes Joshua continued to watch the filming of the attack on the wagon train, until at last, when the sun again dimmed out, the director gave the nod to his assistant, who shouted, "Wrap it up," and shooting was over for the day.

Now came the opportunity for which Joshua had been waiting. His uncle was standing alone, a little apart from the camera crew, watching the quitting-time disorder and the terrier tactics of his assistant to control it. As Tex stood there looking over the widespread scene, Joshua again approached him and this time succeeded in catching his eye. Tex gave him a brief, impersonal glance, looked unconcernedly away, and then turned his head sharply back. Josh stood squarely in front of him with a wide grin on his face. They stared at each other for several seconds, neither one able to speak. Then Tex found his voice.

"Great guns," he fairly shouted, "it's not—it can't be Josh Beacon!"

Joshua nodded his head in grinning affirmation.

"Well, I'll be darned." Tex stepped back, grinning himself now, to get a better look at the boy. In so doing he bumped into a workman who was passing with a large coil of wire slung over one shoulder. The man sidestepped and mumbled apologetically. But Tex did not even hear him. He was so full of the amazing appearance of his nephew that he had to proclaim it to anyone and everyone. "Hey!" he fairly shouted. "This is my nephew Joshua."

"Howdado," said the workman, grinning and awkwardly nodding as he backed away. Tex and Josh looked at each other and laughed.

"Gee, it's good to see you! Where on earth did you come from?"

"We're on our way to California," said Josh. He felt at a loss where to begin a coherent explanation of the events that had led up to this moment.

"Where are your mother and father?" Tex glanced around as he asked the question, evidently expecting to discover them nearby. Returning his gaze to Joshua's face, he was startled to find there an expression of the utmost alarm.

"Good night! I completely forgot."

"Forgot what?" asked Tex.

But Joshua didn't even hear him. With a helpless glance down the gully toward the road and another back at his uncle, he stammered a few semi-coherent words about "getting back," turned away, and began to run.

"Hey! Where you going?" Tex called after him.

"Down to the road. I'll be back." And he was gone.

He sprinted down the flat gully bottom as though he were making a touchdown dash. As he ran he tried to figure out how much time had passed since he had sighted the caravan and strayed away from the road. He had been so completely carried away by all that had taken place that it could just as easily have been ten hours as ten minutes. But as he thought back, step by step, he guessed that it must have been the better part of an hour or thereabouts. His parents certainly must have discovered his absence and turned back for him by this time. Maybe they had even gone by already.

The thought of such a possibility prompted a renewed burst of speed. Maybe they had already gone by, and maybe they hadn't. All he could do now was to get back as quickly as possible to where he should have been.

When he was halfway to the road and within sight of it, he saw a car approaching. It was a shiny blue sedan. He halted for an instant to get a good look at it. From where he stood, hot and panting, it could easily be his parents' car. He began to run again. It would be impossible to reach the road in time so he waved his arm over his head and shouted as he ran, hoping to make himself seen or heard. But as the car sped closer he found himself momentarily cut off from it by the terrain.

It whooshed past within hailing distance, but it was moving too fast for him to make himself heard. When he regained sight of it he could see only a rapidly receding rear end kicking up a cloud of dust through which he thought he glimpsed a yellow and black New York license plate.

He dropped to the ground and sat gasping, his head bent over updrawn knees. When he had caught his breath he arose and paced to and fro by the roadside, mumbling aloud and occasionally kicking out at a weed or pebble. This was a fine fix to have got himself into. It was all his own fault, but what tough luck to have missed them by seconds! And the thing that made it even worse was having missed by such a slim margin that he couldn't be sure whether or not it was really their car which he had seen.

Thus absorbed, he didn't hear the quiet hum of a motor in the gully until it emerged to the roadside and was right behind him. He turned around as it stopped and saw a station wagon. His uncle was at the wheel, and he was leaning across the seat to hold open a door.

Joshua took three long steps and jumped in beside him. "They just went by, I think," he said excitedly. "That way. Maybe we can catch 'em!"

Without hesitation, Tex swung the car onto the road. Not until they were speeding in the direction in which Joshua had pointed did he politely inquire, "Who, may I ask, are we so hotly pursuing?"

V. A Fork in the Trail

Sitting on the edge of the seat beside his uncle, Joshua briefly related all that had happened to him during the past hour. When he had accounted for the peculiar manner of his appearance at the picture-making site and for the abruptness of his departure in search of his parents, Tex appeared considerably reassured. The puzzled look on his face dissolved, and he put himself wholeheartedly into the chase. He tightened his grip on the wheel and pushed the accelerator down to the floor. They had been moving fast before. Now they almost flew.

They were traveling so fast that they sped past the parked car before Joshua realized that it was a familiar blue sedan.

"Did you see that?" he asked, trying to peer back through the swirling cloud of dust.

"No. What was it?"

"A blue car pulled up by the side of the road."

"You think it was the family?"

"I'm not sure. We went by too fast."

"We'd better investigate," said Tex. He took his foot off the accelerator, and the station wagon settled back to earth. They had covered a substantial stretch of road just while exchanging these few words. Now they saw a side road about fifty yards ahead. By the time they reached it Tex had slowed down enough to turn into it, stop, and back out. Facing in the direction from which they had just come, they charged back into their own dust cloud.

The parked car was back about a quarter of a mile. They came to a stop, and Josh got out. Through the settling dust he saw that it was the family car all right. A closer look disclosed that it was parked because of a flat tire. He approached and found his mother and father around back, unloading the trunk to get at the tools. They didn't see him until he was almost beside them.

They were so happy to find him that it was several minutes before either of them noticed his companion, who remained behind the steering wheel, quietly smiling, until Mrs. Beacon looked around and saw him. She recognized him at once. He got out of the station wagon, laughing at her obvious amazement.

There followed a second wave of astonished greetings, incredulous inquiries, and fragmentary explanations more excited than the first. Joy rather than surprise had been the parents' reaction upon seeing Joshua. They were looking for him and they knew that they would find him. But to be unexpectedly confronted by Tex Beacon in the middle of an unpopulated prairie produced a shock as delightful as it was incredible.

While the three older people gave themselves over to an excited exchange of half-questions and unfinished answers, Joshua got out the jack and the lug wrench. He jacked up the wheel that had the flat tire and was taking off the lugs when his father turned to him to say that he would lend a hand in just a minute. Then he was caught back in the verbal rapids, and by the time they had been shot the tire was changed and the tools put away.

The job done, Joshua quietly rejoined the circle of his chattering elders. The afternoon's various adventures had left him dirty and disheveled, and the sight of him served to bring them back to the realization that there were practical matters to be considered.

"Where are you staying?" Mrs. Beacon asked Tex.

"In a little town about five or six miles from where we're working. There used to be a small Army camp just outside it, and some of our crowd are using that. There's a hotel, too, at which I'm staying. Let's get back there and see if we can't find a room for you."

The luggage was restored to the rear trunk, and with Joshua and his mother in one car and the two men in the other they headed for the town. Passing the gully, they encountered a last busload of actors turning onto the road, and ten minutes later they were in the little prairie town which the location crew had temporarily taken over.

The main street, with its old brick hotel and cluster of miscellaneous two- and three-story frame buildings, was predominately peopled with frontiersmen and Indians. Some were on horseback and others were afoot. They were getting out of busses, entering or leaving drugstore and post office, a whole bustling townful of people dressed in the clothes of another era but engaged in modern pursuits, using mannerisms and speech which failed to match their colorful appearances.

In the hotel lobby there were more of them—bearded bullwhackers, buckskin-clad scouts, and painted Indian braves, as well as a number of men and a few women in everyday clothes. Standing or sitting in small groups, chatting together, reading newspapers, smoking cigars and cigarettes, they seemed even more out of place against the potted palms and worn furniture than they did on the street.

Uncle Tex somehow managed to secure a couple of rooms in the crowded hotel, but when it came to enlisting the help of the overworked bellhop he had less luck. This was an exigency, however, which Joshua was quite capable of handling himself. While the rest of the family went upstairs he got the necessary luggage out of the car and brought it into the lobby.

He was so engaged when he saw the old man in buckskins who had been the object of the assistant director's annoyance earlier in the day. Joshua was waiting for the elevator. Across the crowded lobby, through the plate-glass front window, he chanced to notice the man passing in the street.

He was alone, ambling along unhurriedly. Framed in the window, with only a wooden shack and a couple of lounging movie Indians visible in the background, he made a picture so entirely convincing that Joshua forgot for a second both the painful burdens of schoolbook history and the glamorous pretenses of play-acting. As though his own perception were a camera lens coming into focus, he felt that he was looking back a hundred years, out into the street of a frontier settlement. The Indians in the background were visiting savages from an adjacent wilderness. And there passed a frontiersman, a hunter from the plains, or perhaps a trapper from the mountains. His moccasins had trod the forests of the Oregon country, the silent white summits of the Sierra Nevadas, the fragrant valleys of California, and the foreign plazas of Taos and Santa Fe. Then he was gone. An empty bus crossed the picture plane that he had just occupied, and one of the movie Indians on the other side of the street fished a cigarette lighter out from under his blanket. The noise of the lobby rose in harsh crescendo, and the illusion was lost.

The elevator door clanked open, and Joshua crowded in with his suitcases. Slowly rising in the old-fashioned cage, he looked down through the iron grill and watched the carnival drop away. But the picture of the strange old man stayed with him. He couldn't get that tall, lonesome figure with the rich voice out of his mind. He must remember to ask his uncle if he had found out who the man was.

The next morning Joshua went out with his mother and father to watch the shooting. They, of course, took their usual time about breakfast and making ready. He thought they would never get started. When at last they got into the car and drove away from the hotel, the town had been nearly empty for a couple of hours. But when they arrived at the gully the camera was just beginning to roll. It was a sunny morning, and Tex hoped that by quitting time he might have all the footage that was needed on this location.

Mr. and Mrs. Beacon were interested in all that went on, but their enthusiasm could not stand up to Joshua's.

They watched all morning and then went back to town. He watched all day while the camera recorded a variety of views of the caravan crossing the gully and shots of Indians skulking in the offing. Late in the afternoon the assistant director announced that tomorrow all those going back to Hollywood must be ready to leave at seven o'clock in the morning.

It had been a glorious day, but during dinner at the hotel Joshua was morosely silent. His uncle talked casually of the necessity for losing as little time as possible in getting back to the studio, and his parents complacently discussed the balance of their cross-country itinerary.

"I'd like to continue to stick to the old wagon trail as much as possible," said Mr. Beacon.

"Which branch of it are you going to follow on the other side of Dodge City?" asked Tex.

Mr. Beacon looked puzzled. "What d'you mean, which branch?" he asked.

"There were two ways of going," said Tex; "either up over the mountains and through Raton Pass, or south across the Cimarron Desert."

Mr. Beacon weighed this information judiciously before answering. "I think I favor the Cimarron Desert," he decided. Then, turning to his wife, he asked, "Which would you prefer?"

"I'll leave it up to you," she said, "just so long as we can stop over for a week or two in Santa Fe and Taos."

Joshua quietly groaned.

"I'm willing, if you'll agree to stop over at the Grand Canyon and Hoover Dam."

As Joshua glumly listened to his parents' plans, his face grew longer and longer, in direct proportion to the list of possible points of interest between this place and the West Coast. It would be weeks before they got there. The summer would be half over, and it would be almost time to go home. His chances of seeing much more movie-making were becoming distressingly slim.

Over after-dinner coffee the conversation continued in the same vein until Joshua could bear it no longer. He appealed to be excused from the table. But as he was leaving his uncle called him back. "It just occurred to me," he said, "that you might prefer to fly back to L.A. with me tomorrow and spend the time in California that your mother and father are going to spend on the road."

He said it as casually as though he were suggesting another cup of coffee. Joshua hardly dared to believe that he had heard aright. He looked around the table from face to face. Upon each he thought he saw the telltale trace of self-conscious amusement that gives away conspiracies. They had already discussed and decided it, then. He swallowed hard and tried to say something. But for the moment all he could get out was an incredulous "Golly."

VI. The Book

... A hundred years ago America was like a boy growing up, lean and eager, whose voice had changed but who still had a long way to go.

Then, as is sometimes the case with growing youngsters, there came a sudden shooting up and filling out. In a few eventful years an adolescent nation developed from hopeful youth to strapping maturity and stood ready to make a mark in the world.

The history of westward expansion across the North American continent, tumultuously determining the ultimate stature of the United States, is a story of the greatest migration of mankind that has ever been recorded, of a whooping period of rapid growth and national growing pains which reached a climax in the decade of 1840 to 1850 . . . the Roaring Forties.

. . .

With a yawn Joshua let the thick book which he had only just begun reading drop to his lap. He was curled up in a big chair in the living room of his uncle's hilltop house in Los Angeles. Through the glass wall beside him he could look down on the sprawled city and see a myriad of little golden eyes, bright and unblinking in the warm night. It was a splendid view, which included not merely one city but several, for the lights of Pasadena, Burbank, Glendale, and Hollywood were visible from this high place. Having been here only three days, he was not yet sure which part of the widespread area was which, but he did know that those searchlights sticking their beams skyward from behind the western hills were located in the bright streets of Hollywood.

It was late, and Tex was not back from the studio. He had not got home last night until after Joshua was asleep. They had seen each other only in the morning at breakfast. Then the director, contrary to his customary good humor, had seemed distracted and in a hurry.

"The trouble with this business," he had said, "is that

there are too many heads trying to run the show." By way
of further explanation he had merely said that he was tied
up with a bit of unexpected trouble from the "front office,"
which he hoped to have straightened out in a day or two.
He had asked if Joshua would mind waiting until then before coming out to the studio. "Then I'll have a little time
to show you around, and it'll be much better."

It was too bad, of course, but troubles and delays could
not mar Joshua's pleasure in just being here. He was
thrilled by every allusion, whether good or bad, to the
moving-picture industry at work, and now that he was
close to it he could bide his time indefinitely so long as it
meant an eventual introduction behind the scenes.

In the meantime he had been made to feel quite at home
in his uncle's house. And what a wonderful place it was! He
had never been in one like it. To begin with, it was a man's
house, ordinarily occupied solely by Mr. Tex Beacon and
Ben, the West Indian Negro with a dignified British
accent who took care of everything. It was not a big house,
but it gave a feeling of spaciousness because of the wide
windows and glass walls which seemed to merge indoors
with outdoors and took full advantage of the surrounding
vista. Nor was it really a luxurious house, for though it had
every comfort it kept a simplicity which frowned on un-
essentials. The one frank note of luxury was the swimming
pool, and it was so unostentatiously set in an informal gar-
den that it looked as though it had been put there by nature.

So Tex had departed for work with the promise that

tomorrow or the next day they would go to the studio together. As he was leaving the house he had taken a large
volume from a bookshelf and put it in Joshua's hands, saying, "Here's the book on which the picture in progress is
based. You might be interested in looking it over while you
have nothing else to do."

Joshua had intended to spend the day reading it. But
somehow the day had been as fleeting as a pleasant reverie.
The morning sun had called him out for a ramble and then
had insisted that he take a swim in the pool. When Ben
brought lunch out to him on a tray he had been astounded
to learn that half the day was over. And the second half
went wherever the first had gone. In the evening Tex had
phoned to say that he would be late again. So not until
after dinner had Joshua finally managed to get around to
the book.

It was called *Go West*. He had heard it spoken of, for it
had been a best seller, or some such thing, about a year

before. Upon thumbing through it he found to his distress
that it was nothing more nor less than another unadorned
history book. It looked very long and dull. But it was the
basis for the picture he was to witness in the making, so,
history or not, he would have to attempt to read it.

Having settled himself comfortably in a deep chair in
the living room, he conscientiously turned to the introduction. The first thing he read was a note penciled across the
top of the page in his uncle's handwriting: "Historical documentary treatment built around central figures of Kit Carson and John Charles Frémont, the mountain man and the
mapmaker whose joint adventures played a part in forming
the nation. Excitement and action—but *history*, not fiction."

Heartened by the warmth of this personal touch, Joshua
had gone on to the opening paragraphs. At the end of the
second he had yawned. The book sank to his lap, and
his gaze turned to the glitter of distant lights. It was quiet
in the house, and he was beginning to feel sleepy. So many
lights, so many streets and houses and people. Yet up here
it was as silent as the empty prairie. His eyes closed and his
head jerked forward. He forced himself awake and shook
the cobwebs from his brain. He continued to read:

What sort of place was this young country? What did it look
like in those days?

Big for its age, it was lanky, easygoing, and hardly aware
of its own strength. Its past lay cradled in the East—in New

England, Boston, New York, Philadelphia, and in the cultivated acres of tidewater Virginia and the Carolinas. But its individuality was forming with the advance of the inland frontier. In the vigorous communities of the West was to be found the true portrait of America as a promising young land, and the key to its robust personality.

Sturdy and far-spread as was the stripling nation, however, the land it occupied was still too large for it. The western border was merely an imaginary line which could be altered to meet with public convenience. It made no actual barrier between civilization and wilderness. The problem of where and what were the boundaries destined to contain the United States was as perplexing to statesmen at home and abroad as it was to the pioneer homesteader.

Once the Allegheny Mountains had been the wall that backed the seaboard colonies. Their summits and gaps had long since been passed and the fertile lands beyond them plowed and planted. Then the Mississippi River had been crossed and put behind. Now where was the frontier to be? The Rocky Mountains? The Pacific Ocean? It hardly seemed possible.

The wilderness was too vast and hostile to be embraced by a single government. Wanderers who had looked on its secret reaches pronounced it uninhabitable, and their authority stood unquestioned for a generation or more. Only Indians, fur trappers, and a few venturesome traders found it worth while to make human tracks across such wild and inhospitable terrain.

There was developing, nonetheless, an American faction which not only considered it possible, but firmly believed that it was their country's manifest destiny to straddle the continent. If Americans were not going to occupy the potentially rich lands adjoining their mobile western boundary, they would soon find themselves with foreign nations for uncomfortably close neighbors. They would be throwing away numberless opportunities that were yet theirs for the taking. An accumulating mixture of patriotic sentiment and Yankee shrewdness was stirring up a new westward-moving impulse.

Beyond St. Louis, along the banks of the wide, yellow Missouri, the face of the earth was under alteration to suit new occupants. The river was a natural east-west highway as far as the big bend where it wheeled down from the north. Here ended its usefulness to the direct overland traveler bound for the plains and beyond. Here stood the frontier of 1840. At the end of an old road and the outset of a new one a cluster of raw settlements were adding their names to the map. Toward the hustling river towns of Franklin and Independence, Westport and Kansas Landing, moved the people of whom the republic was constituted, the people who were America, the people whose blood and sinew formed blood and sinew of a nation growing . . .

By a determined effort Joshua had managed to negotiate the introduction. But this evening he could hope to go no farther. The weight of his eyelids was becoming too much to resist; at last he fell asleep. The book slipped to the floor. Ben, on the way to his room, picked it up. He put a hand on Joshua's shoulder to wake him so that the boy could go to bed, but he looked so comfortable in the big chair that Ben decided to leave him undisturbed. His uncle could get him up when he came home.

When Joshua was awakened it was by the noise of a door

being opened. That must be Tex, he sleepily concluded. I wonder how long I've been asleep. He listened for footsteps, but there was not another sound. He yawned and stretched. Perhaps he had only dreamed that he had heard his uncle coming home. Then a voice spoke.

"Howdy, lad," it said. It was a very deep voice and sounded just behind him.

Joshua's stomach seemed to turn over, and chills ran down his spine. He jumped to his feet and spun around to find himself face to face with the gaunt old stranger in buckskins whom he had last seen back in Kansas.

VII. The Visitor

"H-how did you get in?" Joshua blurted in a voice that wouldn't behave right.

"Through that door there," answered the old man, pointing a gnarled thumb back over his shoulder. "It was open." His tone and manner were as easy as though he were an expected guest, and he appeared unaware of having given Joshua a bad start. He was dressed in the same frontier outfit that he had been wearing back in Kansas. Standing in the middle of the modern room, he seemed even taller and more rough-hewn than he had out of doors. He held his hat in one hand, and the top of his bald head nearly touched the ceiling.

Yet for all his imposing appearance and the silent suddenness of his arrival, there was something about him that dispelled the boy's alarm almost as soon as it was aroused. Perhaps it was his easy, forthright way, or the rich quality of his voice. At any rate, Joshua found his fears soon giving way to curiosity. Adopting the direct manner of his visitor, he asked him what he wanted.

"I want to talk to the boss," he said.

"You mean Tex? He's not here."

"They tol' me this is where he lives."

"It is," said Joshua, "but he's at the studio."

The old man rubbed his head thoughtfully. "Mind if I squat here a bit an' wait?" he asked.

"Uh—no," answered Joshua. "Have a chair."

"Ruther set on the floor," the man said, and planted himself cross-legged on the carpet near the empty fireplace. From this position he surveyed the room with black eyes squinted against the unaccustomed lights. "Mighty fofurraw fixin's," was his cryptic comment after a careful scrutiny.

Joshua found himself beginning to warm up to this queer old duck. "Say, who are you?" he demanded.

"Name's Meade. Jedediah Meade."

"I see. Well, mine's Josh Beacon. Tex, Mr. Beacon, that is, is my uncle."

"Howdy," said Jedediah Meade.

"Hello," said Joshua.

The brief exchange of salutations was followed by a silence while Meade continued to look around. Joshua was momentarily stumped. How was he going to keep a conversation going without knowing who his visitor was and what he had come here for? And how was he going to find out anything if he could get only terse and noncommittal phrases in answer to his questions?

But having settled himself and become satisfactorily acclimated, the old man ceased his inspection of the room and, to Joshua's surprise, began to talk without any further priming. "A heap of funny things have happened to this old coon," he abruptly announced, "but, scalp my old bald head, this is somethin' new." He paused, deftly rolled and lighted a cigarette, and then continued. "I joined up with this pitcher outfit back in Kansas."

"I saw you back there," said Joshua.

"You did?" The man looked at him as though he were just noticing that he was there. "Well, you're just about the only one what did."

"What do you mean?"

"Well, when they come to town they called me in an' gave me this job. A technical adviser they said I was. Two hundred dollars every week, just to set around. Even if they'd allowed me to do what I was s'posed to be doin', I'd just as soon have done it fer nothin'."

"And what were you supposed to be doing?"

"I was s'posed to be tellin' 'em what the old days was like on the Santa Fee Trail, how the people looked an' talked in those days, an' how the Injuns acted. That's what I was *s'posed* to be doin'. But after the first day nobody paid me no more attention than a prairie dog. I set around an' watched them do everythin' backward like a herd of greenhorns, an' every time I tried to do what they was payin' me to do nobody would listen. I asked to see the boss but I couldn't get near enough to touch him with a coup stick. He seems like a nice enough feller, an' I could see he was tryin' to do everythin' right, but this little coyote what does all the yappin' kept tellin' me the boss was busy. Well, it went on like that fer a week, an' then when they're fixin' to head out fer Californy they made me come with 'em. 'What in thunder d'ye need me fer?' I asked. 'I ain't done nothin' around here yet.'

" 'Ye're on the pay roll, aintchee?' says they. An' they put me on the train an' brung me here. Been a coon's age since I was in Californy. She's sure changed."

"Now that you're at the studio are things any better?"

"I ain't there no more," replied Meade. "Today they tol' me I was fired. Dunno why they brung me all the way to Californy to tell me that. Can't understand those people. Anyhow, I'm headin' back fer Kansas now. I just thought I'd like to see the boss before I go. He seems like a nice feller. I feel like I gotta tell him some of what they gave me all this money fer tellin'."

"I see," said Joshua. "Well, he should be here any time

now. He's been working day and night since he got back."

"Me," said old Meade, "I don't half savvy these movin' pitcher doin's. It's all right to make a pitcher of the old days, I reckon, but if they're so doggone sot on makin' it the way it was, why don't they make it the way it *really* was?"

"What do you mean?" asked Joshua.

"Well, fer instance, they got all about Kit Carson in it. Now when Kit was no more'n knee high to a buffalo calf he ran away from Franklin, Missouri, where he was apprentice boy in a saddler's shop. He joined up with Charlie Bent's spring caravan bound fer Santa Fee. That was away back in the eighteen-twenties when the Santa Fee trade was jest gettin' a good beginnin'. The trail to New Mexico wasn't exactly a trail; it was just the way the wagons went —from Old Palmyra to Willow Springs, from Willow Springs to Council Grove, from Council Grove 'cross prairie to the Arkansas at Great Bend, an' then past Pawnee Rock

to Fort Dodge. Beyond Fort Dodge there was two ways of goin—"

"Either across the Cimarron Desert, or over the mountains by way of Raton Pass," put in Joshua.

"Correct. In those days there weren't no roads west of the Missouri border. There was just prairie an' forest, mountain an' river, desert an' sky. That's all there was, but there was a powerful lot o' them. She was big country, all right, an' she was good country. Outside of the Injuns, traders, an' trappers nobody understood just how good 'til considerable later.

"But Kit Carson now, he knew, all right. He got down to New Mexico an' he liked it good enough to stay. It just smelled right to him up there on the high plateau, an' there was enough room to breathe. He kinda made Taos his home town. He went to work fer Ewing Young, who was in the fur business, an' pretty soon he was a mountain man himself, trappin' beaver all over the West, up an' down the Rockies an' clear out to where we're settin' this minute. When he weren't trappin' he was huntin', like as not, an' when he weren't doin' neither he was fightin' Injuns— either fightin' 'em or makin' friends with 'em. They called him Little Chief, an' he took an Injun squaw. Kit Carson grew up with the West, just about. He had some mighty close scrapes an' some mighty good times. It was fifteen years or thereabouts before he even paid a visit back to the States, an' then he didn't stay around fer long. That was the time he met Lieutenant Frémont."

"Lieutenant Frémont? Who was he?"

"You never heard of Lieutenant Frémont?"

"I guess I've *heard* of him," said Joshua. "But I can't remember exactly who he was."

"Well, he was a young Army fellow from Washington who came West to explore. Course by the time he showed up everythin' had been pretty well explored. But he was a mapmaker. He got Kit Carson an' Tom Fitzpatrick an' some of the other mountain men who knew the West like it was their front yard to guide him through the Rockies an' all over the place."

Jedediah Meade paused reflectively. He had a pleasant, rhythmic way of speaking. He talked like one who had been there and just gotten back. Listening to him was like hearing news rather than history. But it was not only his voice and the way he talked that were so absorbing to Joshua; what he was relating really was news as well as history, for the old man was speaking not only of something that had happened long ago, but also of what was happening right now at the Cosmos moving-picture studio.

Waiting for him to go on, Joshua deliberated whether or not he should try to lead with a question about the picture itself. But before he could put the thought into words the old man was speaking as though he had read his mind.

"They're puttin' it all in the pitcher, so far as I can see," he said. "But still they just ain't got it the way it was. Too fofurraw. Too many fancy trimmin's.

"Now take this squaw of Kit's. She was an Arapaho. But

instead of an Injun woman they got one of these here bathin' beauties from Alabama with some kinda greasepaint all over her face. Scalp my head, she looks about as much like a squaw as I do. There's plenty Injuns around. Why can't they use a genuine one?

"An' the way they got it ye'd think all Kit ever done in the mountains was set in front o' his lodge an' make eyes at his squaw. Wagh! This child don't hold with such doin's.

"Everythin' has to be too nice an' pretty, that's the trouble. Now you take any trapper who's been livin' in the mountains. How d'ye s'pose he looks—like a pretty pitcher? No siree. Like as not you couldn't tell him from an Injun at first look. Or mebbe he's wearin' a buckskin shirt an' coonskin hat. He's been wearin' the same buckskin shirt all winter. He's slept in it, trapped in it, hunted in it, butchered meat in it. So naturally he's beginnin' to look a mite untidy. See what I mean?"

Joshua nodded in thoughtful agreement. The old fellow's talk was making him wonder. What was Tex going to think of all this? After all, he was one of the outstanding directors in Hollywood, and many of his pictures were works of art. A phrase that he had once read in an article about his uncle and always remembered came to Joshua's mind: "Through truth he achieves beauty in a medium where fiction and prettiness are too often the rule."

There certainly was an undeniable logic to Jedediah Meade's criticism. He doubtless knew a lot about the early frontier West. And it was perfectly true that the movies frequently prettied things up too much. But, nonetheless, who was he to tell a director how to film a picture? It looked as though the assistant director had perhaps known what he was doing when he had prevented the old man from speaking to the boss.

Maybe, thought Joshua, it would be sensible for me to do the same thing and try to get rid of him before Tex comes home—if I can think of a polite way to do it.

But the strange visitor again anticipated the boy's words. Yawning and stretching, he rose to his feet. "It's gettin' late," he said abruptly. "It's time this child was makin' tracks."

Joshua was on the verge of saying something about how sorry he was that his uncle was so late, but the old man's disturbing faculty for seeming to know what was on a person's mind before he opened his mouth made him check the impulse. Instead he merely said, "Maybe you can see him some other time."

"I dunno about that," replied Jedediah Meade. "I got no reason fer stayin' around these parts. I'm headin' up the San Joaquin Valley like I done long ago. Take a look at the country an' then make tracks back across the mountains while the weather's still good. This coon's gettin' too old for winterin' in the Rockies."

That's funny talk, thought Joshua. But this was no ordinary individual, and nothing he might do or say could really be surprising. "I'm sorry to hear you're leaving," was all Joshua replied. And he meant it. He liked this venerable, honest backwoods giant. He still didn't know much about him, and his remarks about the picture were somewhat disturbing, but listening to him was as enlightening as reading a history book, and decidedly more entertaining. He was a curious old character but he was good company.

They walked to the door together. Joshua shook the huge rough hand that was offered him and threw back his head to smile a friendly farewell up at the lofty countenance. "I'll tell my uncle you were here," he said. "And I hope I'll see you again."

"Ye can't never tell," declared a receding voice out of the night. "But if ye should it won't be around these parts. No siree. Scalp my head, this child's had enough . . ." And his voice, like his shadowy figure, was lost in the darkness.

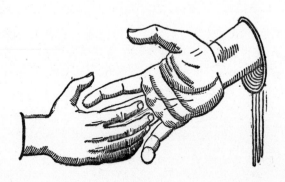

VIII. That's Hollywood for You

Joshua did not see his uncle until the following morning, when he was awakened from a sound sleep by a hand on his shoulder and a hearty voice in his ear. Half opening one eye, he found Tex standing by his bed in the early sunlight. "Wake up, Josh," he was saying. "How would you like to go to work with me today?"

Still only half awake, Joshua was out of bed and into his clothes before Tex, on his way to breakfast, had reached the foot of the stairs. "Fast work," he commented as the boy joined him at the table on the terrace. "You'd make a good fireman."

"Not me." Joshua grinned. "I'm going to be a director."

"Sometimes," his uncle sighed, "I wonder if that's such a good idea."

Joshua glanced at him in surprise. It was not like Tex to make such a remark, even in fun. But it was merely an allusion, Joshua supposed, to the long hours he had been putting in at the studio, and was not to be taken seriously. Tex was tired, no doubt. It showed in his face, and although he was cheerful, as usual, his manner was perceptibly subdued this morning. Joshua wondered at what late hour his uncle had got home last night. The conjecture brought to his mind, for the first time since he had gone to sleep, the visit of old Jedediah Meade. He was on the point of mentioning it when Tex spoke; for the moment the attention of both breakfasters was concentrated on what he had to say.

"I know you must be tired of hanging around the house by yourself and that you're eager to get to the studio, so I'm going to take you with me today. We got back from location a day or two sooner than we expected, and there's been a break in the shooting schedule. But today we get the cameras rolling again."

"How come you've been working so much since you got back if you haven't been shooting?" asked Joshua.

"Well, it's not exactly easy to explain, but I guess I'd better try to, because you're apt to run into the same sort of thing some day if you intend to follow in my footsteps."

Joshua continued his breakfast without even noticing what he was eating. This was the real thing, sitting with a director and listening to his professional problems. This was what he had wanted to come to Hollywood for.

But Tex's next utterance could hardly have been more startling had it been an Indian war whoop. "I've been having a row," he announced, "with my eternal enemy, the front office. The plain truth is that they want to switch directors on the job."

"Switch directors!" Joshua cried in astonishment. "You mean hand the job to another director right in the middle of everything! Why, you're one of the best out here. What would they want to do a thing like that for?"

"Strictly between you and me, just because I am one of the best."

"That doesn't make sense. I don't understand."

"Well, as you know, when I make a picture I want to make the best I possibly can. But that's not always the kind a studio wants."

"They don't want you to make a good picture?" Joshua was completely incredulous. For some reason or other Uncle Tex was turning everything upside down. The boy looked sharply into his face to see if he could be fooling him. But no, the expression he found there clearly told him that this was no joke.

"What *is* a good picture?" Tex shrugged as he answered his own question. "As far as almost any producer is concerned, a good picture is one that makes a lot of money, that makes people willing to stand in lines in the rain to get into the theaters all over the country. And the last two

pictures I've directed have been box-office flops. They lost money."

"B-but I read an article about the last one, telling how it was a work of art, and how you are a great director."

"Sure, but most people who go to the movies don't go looking for great works of art. They go to be entertained."

"I see that," agreed Joshua. "But couldn't pictures be both? I mean, couldn't they be good the way you make 'em, and also entertaining the way people want 'em?"

"Yes," answered Tex, "and that's just what I'm trying to do. But I'm working with two strikes against me because my pictures are losing money. The front office is afraid that I might be making this one too arty, and that it will be a flop too. Mr. Beckett, who is the producer of this picture, and who also produced the last one I directed, is worried."

"Is he the one who wants to change directors?"

"No, he doesn't want to see me go. He and I have our differences sometimes, but usually we work together pretty well. But he's responsible for the success of the production, and he has to make sure that the vice-presidents in the front office and the bankers back in New York are satisfied. Their chief concern is making money, and they're the ones who want him to get another director. All he wants is to be sure that I make the kind of horse opera that will go over in a big way."

"What's going to happen?" Joshua asked the question with such solemn concern that his uncle had to smile.

"I don't exactly know, Josh, but don't you worry too much. I'm going to continue to do the best I possibly can, and if they just don't interfere with me until I've finished this job, I hope that I can turn out a picture that will satisfy everybody."

He paused for a moment, lost in thought. Then, abruptly getting up from the table, he said, "The only reason I've let you in on all this is because I want you to know the kind of problems a director comes up against. And now that you know what the fuss is all about we'd better be taking ourselves out to the studio or they *will* get another director."

They said good-by to Ben, got into the car, and wound down the road that descended steeply from the hilltop to a broad parkway. Riding through the morning traffic, Joshua pondered what he had just heard.

It all added up to something of a blow. The moving-picture business was not quite as simple as he, in his blind enthusiasm, had presumed it to be. Hundreds of thousands of dollars—even millions—were spent to make a picture which, in turn, made a great many more. But apparently there were some pictures that didn't make money. He had never thought of that. And it had never occurred to him that so many different people were involved, and that such conflicts of personalities and ideas existed. His uncle was an important director, and Joshua had always supposed that when Uncle Tex made a picture he had laid down the law. But there was much more to it than that. There were many others with their fingers in the pie, with their own interests and ideas, each having a different degree of authority.

Some of the remarks that Jedediah Meade had made about the picture the previous evening began to come to mind. At the time he had thought that maybe they were just the cranky criticisms of an eccentric old man, but now he began to see them in a new light. Maybe there was something to them, and perhaps they would be of interest to his uncle. With this thought came the realization that he had not yet gotten around to mentioning his midnight visitor.

"Gee," he abruptly exclaimed, "I was about to tell you a little while ago, and then all you said made me forget. Someone came to see you last night—that old fellow from Kansas."

"What old fellow from Kansas?"

"A tall old man in a long buckskin shirt. He was a technical adviser, hired back in Kansas. He wanted to see you."

"Oh, yes," said Tex. "I remember the one. What on earth did he want?"

"He just wanted to talk, I guess. He told me all about how he was hired when you were on location, and then no sooner was he hired than nobody paid any more attention to him. But they made him come out to Hollywood because he was on the payroll, and then they fired him."

"Humph," said Tex. The sound was a sort of humorless chuckle. "That's Hollywood for you all right. I suppose he was looking for me to tell me off."

"No," Joshua said, "that couldn't have been why he came. He's a strange old fellow but he seems pretty nice. He said that he was paid to give advice, and there were a few things he thought he ought to tell you before he left. He calls you 'the boss.' "

"He sounds like the only honest man in Hollywood. Did he say just what sort of things he wanted to tell me?"

"Yes, he stayed and talked for quite a while. He told me a lot about the old days in the West. He sounded as if he'd been there. And he thought that the trouble with the picture was that it made everything too pretty and nice compared to the way it really was. He certainly seemed to know what he was talking about."

"I wonder if he'll be around again." The director's attention was focused on the problem of maneuvering his car across a congested intersection, but at the same time he was obviously interested in what his nephew was saying. "It sounds to me as if he knows what he's talking about. He might be someone who should have been made better use of while there was the chance."

"He said he was going away, something about heading up the San Joaquin and back across the mountains before winter sets in. He's certainly an odd guy. But I liked hearing him talk. He had a nice voice and sometimes he sounded almost like he was reciting poetry. Only it wasn't poetry; it was real talk that made everything he said seem important and as if it had actually happened."

Joshua's remarks set Tex thinking. He drove in silence, a slight frown wrinkling his forehead, his mind obviously on his problems at the studio. The boy too was lost in thought, or rather in puzzled conjecture, for so many things were turning out to be entirely different from what he had expected.

But after a few minutes, as they rounded a wide curve and came upon an open suburban landscape with houses and trees sparsely scattered over a flat plain, Joshua's attention was diverted from his musings to a conspicuous group of hangar-like buildings encircled by a high wooden wall. Of one thing he was suddenly certain: there stood a moving-picture studio.

IX. The Studio

COSMOS PICTURES. The words stood in bold letters high over the triple arches of the entrance. Lofty wrought-iron gates were thrown wide to an inflow of morning traffic. Joshua felt the kind of glowing excitement he had sometimes experienced at the theater, waiting in his seat for the lights to dim and the curtain to rise.

Armed policemen stood guard at the gate, checking the identities of those who wished to enter. "Good mornin' to ye, Mr. Beacon," said one, and with a nod to Joshua grinningly added, "Are ye sure it's quite all right to be lettin' *him* in?"

"Sure it's all right, Pat. This is my nephew."

"Then all right it must be," the guard jovially asserted and waved them through the central archway.

"It's almost like entering an Army camp in wartime," commented Joshua.

"Everybody wants to get in to see how movies are made," said Tex. "We wouldn't be able to work if we let them all in."

Once past the guarded gate it was more like a triumphal entry into a fabulous walled city. On either hand loomed the mysterious façades of the huge windowless edifices that were the sound stages, and beyond their massive corners were fragmentary promises of many other

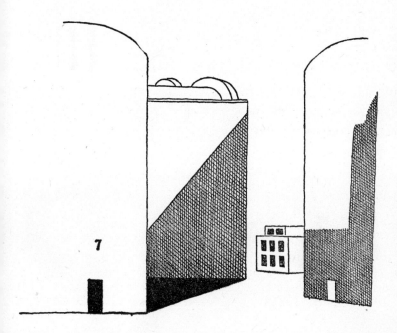

structures, ranging in size from bungalows to office buildings. Trucks and automobiles rolled through the wide
streets, and at a busy corner a policeman was directing
traffic.

Tex parked the car in front of a little sign which bore
his name. They got out and walked between the buildings.
From a carpenter shop could be heard hammering and
the busy whine of a buzz saw, and from a row of bungalows
came the sounds of various musical instruments. Alongside
the walks grew trees and hedges and flowers. Everything
was neatly groomed and pleasant to look at. Men and
women going to their work exchanged greetings and remarks as they passed one another. Some were actors in
costume and make-up, some were workmen in overalls,
and others were just people in ordinary business clothes
who looked much like people going to work in New York
or almost any other American city.

"The first thing I usually do in the morning," said Tex,
"is stop by the producer's office to check with him before
getting to work. I'd like you to meet him."

He led the way up the front steps of a centrally located
official-looking building, which was obviously the home
of the front office. Here Joshua was conducted to a room
where he met a ruddy-faced man with horn-rimmed spec-
tacles who sat, his hat still on his head, at a desk by a large
window. This was the producer, Mr. Robert Beckett.

His manner, at first impression, seemed brusque, almost
rude. Introductions and morning preliminaries were brief,

and the two men lost little time in getting down to business. Left to himself, Joshua turned to a table that held a small model of a set. It represented the deck of some kind of old-fashioned steamboat; although it claimed his close attention, he could not help overhearing the conversation taking place across the room.

"We begin shooting again this morning," he heard Tex saying. "I've penciled a few suggestions on the margins of this script. I'd like you to take a look at them."

Mr. Beckett took the script. There was a short silence while he glanced over it. Then he handed it back, shaking his head. "No changes, Tex. You'll have to leave it as is."

"But look, Bob. There are just a few things that could still be done to the last part of this picture that would make a big difference in the quality and certainly wouldn't hurt anybody."

Mr. Beckett sat there with his hat on, shaking his head in silent negation.

"It's a picture about history," insisted Tex, "but it's not historically right."

"If we stick to cut-and-dried history," said Mr. Beckett, "we won't have much of a picture. This part you want to change, especially, would be just a lot of long-winded, uninteresting talk."

"That's where you're wrong. It's possible to dramatize what really happened and make it even more exciting and interesting than all this claptrap horse-opera stuff about beautiful señoritas swooning in the arms of Kit Carson."

"Well, I know what you mean," the producer said, "but I can't do it. This picture *has* to make money. We're stuck with a historical, and the best way we can be sure of putting it across is to make it look like just another Western. If I had my own way about it I'd be willing to take the chance and do as you say. But as it is—"

"You wouldn't be taking a chance," Tex curtly declared.

"All right. But I can't let you do it. If I do, they're ready to make me put another director on the job, as you know. And if that were to happen there wouldn't be enough left of our picture to stand a chance at the box office or any place else. There are only a few more weeks left on this job. Let's get it over with. If it turns out a success, you'll be free to do the next one the way you want it."

The producer's tone was firm. Joshua looked up from the

model set, startled to find himself witnessing a quarrel between two irate men. But to his relief Tex made no further
argument. Glancing at his watch, he merely said, "I'd better
get over to the set. I'm late already." Then, with a hand on
the doorknob, he paused to add, "At least I hope you're
right about the next one. Somebody has to try to make a
better picture once in a while. That's the only way the
industry has gotten where it has. Come along, Josh."

"Why not leave him here if you're in a hurry?" Mr. Beckett said. "I'll show him around a bit." The dispute having
been disposed of to his satisfaction, his manner had re-
laxed and assumed a warmth which had hitherto not been
apparent. Joshua hardly felt enthusiastic about the idea but
he kept his sentiments to himself. Under the circumstances
it was a convenient suggestion and was quickly agreed
upon.

Tex departed, and a minute later Joshua could see him
through the window, striding energetically away along the
sunny walk. The producer too sat looking thoughtfully
after him. "Best director in the business," he suddenly exclaimed. "But I have to hold him back all the time. He's a
bit ahead of us all."

This remark, coming so soon after the sharp words Mr.
Beckett had just been exchanging with Tex, took Joshua
by surprise. Mr. Beckett noticed the puzzled expression
that passed across the boy's face. He smiled slightly but
said nothing.

Then Joshua smiled too. Mr. Beckett was all right. "It

must be because I'm new around here," Joshua said. "Nothing seems to make sense this morning."

"Then let's try to get you better acquainted right away," said the producer quickly. "Where would you like to begin?"

"If it's not asking too much," said Joshua, "I'd like to begin at the beginning."

Mr. Beckett grinned. "That's not the way we usually do things, but it won't hurt to try." He got up from behind his desk and led the way out of the office. "This picture we're doing now," he said as they walked along, "is scheduled to be shot in about forty days. But we began working on it nearly six months before we were ready to shoot. Do you realize how much effort is put into a picture before it goes in front of the cameras?"

"Well," answered Joshua, "I know that there must first be a story, and that the story must be written into a script, and that the cast must be chosen and the costumes and sets designed and made."

"That's right. Those are some of the main things. But every last detail of the entire production must be planned and organized before even an inch of film is exposed. It's a big job and it takes a lot of people. Now *Go West* is a historical picture. A lot of research had to be done before sets or costumes were designed. So the first thing I'm going to show you is our research department."

They had crossed the street and were entering a building directly opposite Mr. Beckett's office. Inside was a

library with all the studious atmosphere of the schoolroom. Books and maps and filing cases occupied every available foot of space in a high-ceilinged main hall. A tall gray-haired woman got up from a book-littered table and stepped forward to greet them. "This is Mrs. Horseman, our research director," said Joshua's guide. "You can ask her anything you want to know, from how deep is the Great Salt Lake to what color were Cleopatra's eyes; and if she doesn't know the answer she'll manage to find it for you somehow, somewhere."

Mrs. Horseman was an enthusiastic woman, with whom eagerness to be of service was a long-standing habit. When she learned that Joshua was Mr. Beacon's nephew and that he had an especial interest in pictures, she lost no time in hustling him from Mr. Beckett's custody to an alcove where the reference material for *Go West* was gathered.

Here, in addition to shelf upon shelf of books, were collected faded pioneer diaries, maps, and old engravings.

As the research director explained, this was the nearest thing obtainable to a complete record of the opening of the American Far West. She pointed out material on the Santa Fe Trail, on the fur trappers who first explored the Rockies in their prodigious quest for beaver pelts, on the Indians of the plains and mountains, on Frémont and his three survey expeditions made between 1840 and 1850, on the migrations of settlers to Oregon and California in the same period, and on the gold rush of 1849.

In her enthusiasm she bombarded Joshua with information until his head was spinning. From behind a sheaf of papers that had been thrust under his nose he cast an appealing glance toward Mr. Beckett, only to discover him on the far side of the room being summoned to a telephone. He could see him listening for a short time and putting the instrument down. Then he was recrossing the room, and deliverance was at hand.

But to Joshua's dismay the producer hurriedly announced that he had been called to his office for a minute. He was gone before the boy could think of any tactful way to plead for release from Mrs. Horseman. There was nothing for him to do but continue to glance from one to another of the volumes and papers which she piled in front of him and murmur, "How interesting," or, "Is that so."

Ten or fifteen minutes passed so slowly that they seemed

like an hour. This was hardly what he had expected a visit
to a studio to be like. He began to worry. What if Mr. Beckett had become so busy that he had forgotten him? How
should he go about escaping from this predicament?

The researcher's voice went on at a rate he could no
longer keep up with. He looked at the things she showed
him, stifled his yawns, and pretended to listen to her, but
he hardly heard or saw any more than an occasional word
or phrase—until a piece of paper bearing the name J.
Meade happened to catch his attention. From bored in-
difference he suddenly became all eyes and ears.

". . . and this list," Mrs. Horseman was saying, "in-
cludes every man who is known to have been with Frémont on any of his expeditions. Wherever anything is
known about the appearance of the individual a description is included after the name."

There it was at the bottom of the page—just the name
J. Meade, without any further comment. Joshua eagerly
scanned the dozen pages that comprised the list in the hope
of finding some explanation of who this Meade might have
been. Holy cow, he excitedly declared to himself, maybe he
was some relation to old Jedediah Meade. Maybe it was
his father or his grandfather.

He asked Mrs. Horseman if she could tell him anything
about the man who bore this name. Gratified to perceive
that her visitor was finally showing some signs of interest
in her department, she became like a hound in sight of

the quarry. Together they began to go diligently through card indexes, bibliographies, and manuscripts to find, if possible, exactly who this J. Meade might have been. The minutes that had been dragging so tediously for Joshua flew unnoticed until more than half the morning was gone.

But search as they might, it eventually became apparent that the identity of this particular frontiersman was going to be difficult, perhaps impossible, to establish. At last the research director, a little of the edge gone from her initial enthusiasm, had to admit that the reason the list gave no more information was very probably because no more was on record. She promised to let Joshua know if anything should turn up, and as they sat resting from their efforts she inquired why he was so interested in the name J. Meade.

Joshua, puzzling as to whether he might have made an exciting discovery or merely come across a coincidence of names, answered thoughtlessly, "Oh, because I happen to know him." Then, as he noticed that she was regarding him wonderingly, he smiled at his own absent-mindedness and began to explain further. "You see I met a man who—"

But at this moment Mr. Beckett hurriedly reappeared and interrupted with a profuse apology for having been gone so long. It was, he astonishingly pointed out, almost noon. They must hurry if they were going to see any more before lunch. Without giving the boy time for more than an abbreviated thank you and good-by to Mrs. Horseman, he rushed him out of the library, leaving the research director, smudged and a little disheveled from her morning's efforts, looking perplexedly after them over the top of a pile of books.

"We'll just have time to stop by the art department," said Mr. Beckett. "The art directors are just about the best customers the library has. You'll see how the source material which Mrs. Horseman and her assistants have collected is next transformed into visual terms. I think you'll find it a little more interesting than research."

"The research department was pretty interesting," said Joshua. "I want to go back there sometime. I didn't have time to find out everything I'd like to know."

Mr. Beckett gave Joshua a sharp look. "Well," he commented, "you *are* interested in all angles of this picture business, aren't you?"

It was the kind of question that doesn't need an answer.

Jessie
Frémont

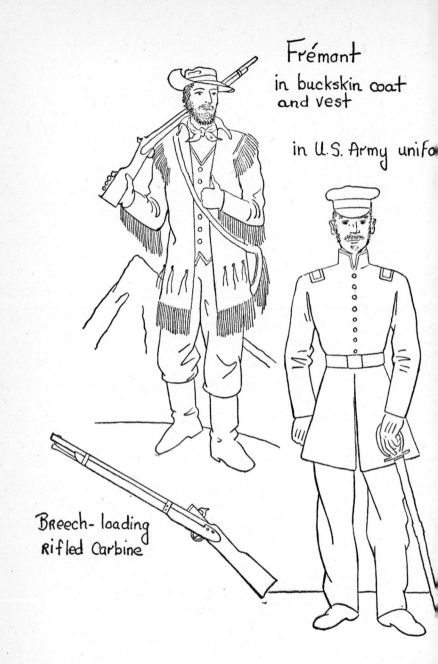

Frémont
in buckskin coat
and vest

in U.S. Army unifo

Breech-loading
Rifled Carbine

Mountain Men in buckskins

FRONT OF SHIELD

Scalps

Comanche Brave

Dress made from two whole
deer skins sewn together

Squaw

X. The Cameras Roll

The noon hour ended Joshua's visit to the art department, and in the company of Mr. Beckett and one of the art directors he was on his way to the commissary to meet Tex for lunch.

As they drew near the restaurant they became part of a converging crowd of studio personnel strolling leisurely to their meal. Here, observed Mr. Beckett, was the only place where a large proportion of all those employed on the sixty-acre lot ever gathered together at one time.

Entering the huge dining room were men and women in evening clothes, cowboys with hats pushed back on their

heads and spurs jingling on their boots, and United States soldiers in old-fashioned uniforms. Seated together at one table, talking and laughing, were a ragged, unshaven tramp, a woman wearing an elegant gown, and a minstrel man in blackface, while at another a group of frontiersmen and Indians in the costumes Joshua had just seen drawings for were quietly chatting over dessert and coffee.

Among the actors and actresses he was able to recognize several well-known faces. It was odd to see the owners in person, for after one had been long accustomed to their images on the screen the living persons seemed, somehow, like marvelously realistic imitations of their familiar movie shadows.

As soon as Tex arrived the four of them found a table and sat down together. Joshua was anxious to tell his uncle how he had come across the name J. Meade in the research library. Surely this knowledge would be as exciting to the director as it was to him. If it should turn out that the old man who had recently been employed on this lot was a close relative of the J. Meade who had been with Carson and Frémont, his grandson perhaps, he might be of value to the studio. Last night, when old Meade had come out to the house, he had talked of the frontier West with an impressive authority for which he evidently had good reason. And now, Joshua thought, he knew why.

Excited as he was, however, to have found reason for suspecting that the astonishing old man who called himself Jedediah Meade was in some way linked to the background story and history which formed the basis for the picture, he could see that this was not the right time or place to talk about it. The three executives quite obviously wanted to forget about their work and relax for a few minutes. Their conversation ran to small talk about golf, family, and a fishing trip that Mr. Beckett was planning for his vacation. While they chatted amiably, Joshua quietly ate his lunch, thought about his discovery, and watched the colorful scene around him. When the meal was finished Tex was the first to rise from the table and declare himself ready to get back to work. "Are you coming with me this afternoon?" he asked his nephew.

Joshua most certainly was. So they said good-by to the

other two men and left the commissary. "We're working
on Stage Seven over there." Tex pointed to one of the great
windowless structures that stood near the gate through
which they had entered earlier in the day. "I wanted to get
back early enough so that I'd have time to make you feel
at home before the afternoon's shooting gets under way."

Striding along beside his uncle, Joshua found no chance
to tell him about the morning in the research library. It
would have to wait until after work.

They hurried past others who had finished lunch and
were drifting back to their respective places. They approached the sound stage and passed through its concrete
side by way of a thick door that looked like the insulated
door of some huge icebox.

Inside was a narrow vestibule and still another sound-
proof door, which admitted them to a place that seemed at
first to be a vast void, without light and weirdly silent. But
when Joshua had readjusted his eyes to the change from
sunlight to gloom he found himself peering up at the
padded inner surfaces of the same towering walls and lofty
roof that he had just been looking at from the street. Their
function was simply to enclose a soundless and unlighted
area, a dim space in which Joshua's eyes were gradually
able to discern the forms of various props and sets. Over
there was the front of a stately porticoed mansion surrounded by lawn and trees, all full-size yet occupying only
a corner of the great interior. When he became better able
to see he realized that there were other sets looming dim

and deserted on the spacious floor. Gawking in all directions as he followed his uncle, he saw a sumptuous interior consisting of several large, handsomely furnished rooms. Not a detail was lacking, and the effect was so completely realistic that only the absence of ceilings reminded him that this was not an actual residence he was looking into. The top of the set was open. Scaffoldings thrust their shadowy crisscrosses up into the darkness, and the black forms of cold lights of many shapes and sizes were visible over the tops of the walls.

At the far end of the great sound stage was still another set, toward which they seemed to be heading. A light came on before they reached it, and Joshua perceived that there were a number of people gathered around the steamboat deck for which he had already seen the model and the sketches.

These people proved to be some of the actors and technicians, who were beginning to get back to the set from lunch. As the noon hour was drawing to an end, electricians were fooling with their lights, turning them off and on and adjusting them. A man stepped up to the microphone at the end of a long boom that stuck out over the deck and began to say, "Sound test, one, two, three, four," over and over again.

"The scene we're working on today," Tex explained, "takes place aboard a steamboat bound up the Missouri River from St. Louis to the frontier in the spring of the year eighteen forty-two."

"Did I miss much by not being here this morning?" inquired Joshua anxiously.

"Very little. We rehearsed and did a few takes, but we'll be doing exactly the same thing over and over again all afternoon."

Tex got Joshua a chair and showed him where he could sit so that he would be able to see all that went on and at the same time be out of the way. Then, as more and more people were gathering around, he tried to point out who was who and some of the features Joshua might be interested in looking out for. Two or three faces he recognized from the location crew back in Kansas. There was the busy little assistant director, dressed as nattily as ever, rushing around giving orders. And the men taking their places at the camera, Joshua remarked to his uncle, also seemed familiar.

"Yes," said Tex, "they were on location in Kansas. The one with the mustache is Bud Shore, the cameraman. The tall blond chap behind the camera is the second cameraman. He's the man who actually operates the camera. The other one is the assistant, who checks the focus and looks after the film and the camera's general well-being."

"Well, gee whiz," broke in Joshua. "What on earth does the cameraman do if his assistants take care of everything that has to do with working the camera?"

"He is the artist," explained Tex, "who spells the all-important difference between good and bad photography. His tools are the camera lens and the lights. He's worked with the art director from the beginning of the production, figuring out the lighting for each shot so that actors and sets would photograph in the way best suited to the story. While we are shooting he sticks close to the lens and tries to see the scene just as the camera does. I could make movies without my good right hand, but I couldn't get along without a good cameraman, and Bud Shore is one of the best."

Joshua felt a bit foolish. He should have stopped to think. Of course the cameraman had enough to do without worrying about the mechanics of working the camera. It was not hard to see, when you thought about it, that next

to the director he doubtless played the most important part in filming a picture.

But Tex was pointing out the other key workers and explaining their responsibilities. There was no time for Joshua to worry about his blunders if he intended to keep up with what was going on. Nearby was the sound engineer, seating himself at his complex wheeled console and putting on the headphones through which he would be listening to the sound in order to control it. "He is connected by telephone to the recording room, which in this case is four blocks away from here," explained the director. "When we are ready to begin shooting he will be the man to signal the recording room, and they will push the button that starts the camera rolling."

"Maybe I sound dumb," said Joshua, "but why does somebody four blocks away start the camera when there are three men seated right beside it?"

"It's another one of those things that sound funny but really make sense when you think about it. The camera is started by the recording man, you see, so that he can get it running at exactly the same speed as his recording equipment—"

A man stepped up to the director to interrupt with a question about some detail and then hurried away. Tex informed Joshua that he was called the "unit man." It was his duty to coordinate the various departments to see that no blanks were ever left where one person's responsibilities ceased and another's began. It was an important job in an enterprise that involved so many people doing so many different things. Tex pointed out the chief electrician, called the "gaffer," and his assistant, the "best boy." Over there was the property man, checking the set to make sure everything was in its proper place, and there was the "grip," a skillful troubleshooter who was on hand to fix anything that might get out of order. There was the script clerk taking her seat close to the scene of action. It was her job to keep careful notation of the details of speech, action, make-up, and costume in every scene as it was acted, so that whenever another part of the same scene was shot at a later date—in some instances several weeks later—these important details would not fail to match.

"And over there," Tex finally said, "do you see that empty chair?"

Joshua craned his neck and solemnly nodded.

"Well, that's the director's seat, and if you watch closely you'll see him take his place in just a few seconds."

With a smile he was gone, leaving the boy to watch the last-minute preparations and figure out for himself what was happening. The whole area was now busily peopled, and Joshua could sense the air of mounting tension. There could be no doubt that something important was about to take place.

At last the actors were moving onto the set. There were fourteen or fifteen of them—frontiersmen in fringed buckskin; rough-looking rivermen; a scattering of elegant gentlemen wearing long sideburns and stovepipe hats; a few

Indians wrapped in blankets; two or three women with voluminous skirts, feathered bonnets, and frilly parasols. The last actor to take his position was resplendent in blue and gold, a handsome black-haired young Army officer. A make-up man followed him onto the set, putting final touches to his face, like a portrait painter unwilling to part with his finished masterpiece.

And now the noise and bustle were subsiding. A few last-minute thoughts caused a scamper and flurry here and there. Then the disorder and preparatory milling about were over. A voice shouted, "Hit 'em!" and the lights blazed on.

In a dazzling flash the shadowy set turned into a section of the narrow deck of an old steamboat, crowded with frontier travelers. The planks underfoot were realistically smooth and worn. A wisp of dark smoke drifted down, as though blown from the stack of a moving steamer.

"Quiet, please!" demanded the voice of the assistant director. A whistle blew, and such a tremendous silence fell over the great sound stage that Joshua was hesitant to so much as swallow for fear the noise might reverberate from wall to wall.

"Let 'em roll!" called Tex's voice.

Joshua could see the sound engineer tinkering with his complicated board. A light flashed on, and he looked up to call out, "Speed!" The recording equipment and the camera were running together at a synchronized speed.

"Action!" said the director.

XI. A Take

The deck of the steamboat was like a long, shallow porch with a wooden railing in the foreground, a low roof overhead, and the doors and windows of staterooms in a row in back. The handsome young Army officer leaned on the rail, looking darkly down over the boat's side. Other passengers stood nearby, or strolled back and forth, sometimes passing behind him.

The buckskin-clad figure of a compact, weathered looking man with long sandy hair showing beneath his broad-brimmed hat sauntered to the rail near where the Army officer leaned and stood looking down toward the water.

They paid no attention to each other; one seemed deeply absorbed by his own thoughts and oblivious of all else, while the other showed an easygoing curiosity in everything around him and no one thing in particular.

While the two men were standing near each other a burly fellow wearing the peaked black cap of a steamboat man came striding along the deck behind them. As he was about to pass the frontiersman he hesitated, went on a few steps, then stopped and backed up, bending this way and that all the while in an attempt to get a better look at the averted face. After a few seconds' further hesitation he reached out a big paw, tapped the buckskin shoulder, and stepped to the rail between the frontiersman and the thoughtful Army officer.

"You ain't named Kit Carson, by any chance?" he demanded in a deep, rough voice.

"That's what they call me," the frontiersman answered.

"Blow me down!" roared the other. "Dontcha 'member me—Will Allen? I used to bring my daddy's harness into Workman's shop in Franklin when you was a 'prentice boy there. Must uv been fourteen or fifteen years ago."

Kit Carson looked him over calmly. "Sixteen," he said with a sudden grin, sticking out his hand. "Sho 'nuff, I remember. You used to be sort of a fat boy. Yore pap was a mule skinner an' took you down to Santa Fee."

"Tha's right. An' I liked to died on the desert. Now I'm a river pilot. It's more to my likin'. Whar you been all these years?"

"I run away from Workman," said Kit Carson, "an' went down to Santa Fee too. But me, I kinda liked it down there."

"An' you been thar ever since?"

"There, an' all over. This is my first trip back to the States since I run away from the saddle shop. Just been to St. Louis. Wagh! I'm headin' back West an' I'm in a hurry."

"Whatcha goin' to do when you get out thar?"

Kit shoved his hat back and scratched his head. "Dunno for sure. Beaver ain't worth trappin' no more since all the dandies begun wearin' them silk stovepipes." He gave his own wide hatbrim a yank and dropped his hand with a slap to his leather-covered thigh. "Shucks," he said, "that's a dern fool question. Mebbe I'll hunt buffalo for the Bents'

outfit like I was doin' before, an' mebbe I'll settle down for a bit an' try some farmin' like I always wanted to do. Anyways, I'll be able to figger it a heap better when I get there."

The Army officer had straightened up from his musings and turned with interest toward the men talking at his elbow. Now the steamboat pilot noticed him for the first time and recognized him. "Howdy, Lieutenant," he said in his jovial manner.

"Good morning, Captain," said the Army officer.

"Lieutenant, do you know Kit Carson?"

"I don't believe I've had the honor," the lieutenant replied.

"Kit, this is Lieutenant Carson. He's a-headin' out West too."

"Cut it!" broke in the director's voice from the shadows in front of the set. The man playing the part of the river pilot had unconsciously said "Carson" when he meant "Frémont" and thereby spoiled the take. Tex got up from his chair and climbed onto the deck. He talked quietly to the three actors who grouped around him to hang on his every word. Joshua could not make out what he was saying but he could tell from his gestures that he was going through some of the action and making corrections.

There was a general flurry of movement as nearly everybody took advantage of the interlude to relax for a moment or to check equipment or exchange a few words. The make-up man was fussing with the lieutenant again, while he, in turn, was listening to the director. The script clerk was making notes, and the other actors were smoothing their costumes, clearing their throats, and wiping from their faces the beads of perspiration caused by the hot lights.

When Tex returned to his seat the actors got back in position to begin again. As Joshua watched the scene for a second time it occured to him that what he was seeing and hearing was the same meeting between Carson and Frémont that old Jedediah Meade had been telling him about last night. Here the remote facts that the old man had spoken of were coming to life before his eyes. A recognizable picture was forming in his mind, like a picture puzzle when enough of the pieces have been put in place. And along with recognition came a sensation of mounting excitement, the thrill of discovery. It was akin to the feeling aroused by the discovery of the name J. Meade in the library. For the first time the jumble of historical fragments with which Joshua had been pestered since leaving home were falling into a pattern, and for the first time he felt that he really believed and *knew* something that had taken place long ago.

Kit Carson was the fellow who had run away from Franklin, Missouri, with a caravan bound down the Santa Fe Trail, and had made good in the West. No longer was it just an empty fact. And Lieutenant Frémont was a handsome Army officer who led survey parties and explored the uncharted Western wilderness. The men in front of the

camera were only actors, to be sure, but through them he could at last believe in the historic personages they were portraying.

It was a kind of inspiration to Joshua. It felt good to know that you knew something, even though it was only a little bit. Now he could better sympathize with his uncle's concern for making a picture that would be authentically historical rather than "just another Western." And for his own part, watching the scene being filmed, he could better understand what was happening, and even anticipate what was going to happen, now that he had some idea of the whole story.

"Cut!" Again the sharp command interrupted the proceedings. It interrupted his musings too, Joshua realized.

His revelation had transported him off into a daydream. Now he noticed that a number of glances were directed toward him. He felt his cheeks warming with embarrassment as the awful thought struck home that it was he who was responsible for this interruption. Unconsciously he had been moving about in his chair. His legs were in a different position from the way they had been a few minutes before. He must have made some sound that the microphone had picked up, and it was he who had spoiled the take.

Shrinking down in his chair, he was grateful for the darkness in which he was seated. Miserably he wondered what was going to happen. But to his relief he soon perceived that if the director, or anybody else, did know exactly where the sound had orginated, nothing was going to be said about it publicly. Everybody was acting as though this little accident were nothing more nor less than one of the difficulties of the day's work. It was taken as something to be expected, and the break was used for further direction and instruction.

The scene was begun again. This time Joshua made sure to keep his wits about him and his feet in one spot. And this time all went well. The scene was enacted in its entirety, and camera and microphone recorded it to the satisfaction of the director, the cameraman, and the sound engineer.

As Joshua was able to anticipate, the balance of the scene consisted of a lively conversation between Frémont and Carson, which revealed that the Army officer was troubled because the guide who had been engaged to accompany him to the South Pass of the Rockies had failed to show up. Kit Carson was at liberty, and as it seemed that nobody could claim to know the mountains any better than did he, it was agreed that he fill the place of the missing guide. The matter being settled, the lieutenant cheered up considerably and the scene came to an amiable conclusion.

After the successful take was completed a few adjustments were made in the lights and the entire procedure was successfully gone through once more. Then there was a break while the camera was moved to a new position and further changes were made in the lights.

The same scene was to be shot again from a different angle. Everybody was moving about, shifting equipment, and changing position. Tex and the cameraman were consulting with the lighting foreman, who was calling instructions to his assistants. "Hang another baby over there!" he would shout. Then another spotlight would be placed over the set and tested. "Okay. Break its neck!" This violent injunction was complied with by a nimble assistant, who merely placed a white shade in front of the spot to diffuse its light. "That's good. Hold it!"

And so, to Joshua's delight and fascination, it went. This was the business, the sweat and the lingo and the excitement of making a moving picture. What could compare with it? Who, with an ounce of sense in his head, would want to do anything else? Not Joshua Beacon, come what might.

While he stood by his chair, taking it all in, the script clerk caught his eye and beckoned to him with a friendly smile. "Have you seen what the script looks like?" she asked.

No, he had not yet got around to that. She gave him a copy to look at during the break. He took it to his place and began to thumb through it by the half-light which now fell on the area.

He was able to find the scene which he had just seen photographed, and he glanced over it. There, word for word, was the dialogue to which he had just been listening. Accompanying it was a running description of the action. Each change of camera position, he noticed, was designated as a scene and was successively numbered. Camera positions were indicated by the terms close shot, medium shot, and long shot. He turned with interest to the pages following the present scene and began to read, to learn what was going to happen.

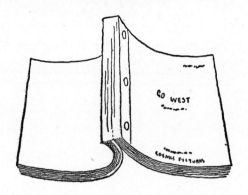

XII. The Script

FADE IN

SCENE 27—CLOSE SHOT INTERIOR. DINING TABLE. Still life of heavy silver, a linen napkin, a sparkling plate, and a crystal glass. The chair at the place is empty. CAMERA slowly moves back.

SCENE 28—MEDIUM SHOT. DINING TABLE. CAMERA pans around table to show, one after another, the members of the household finishing their meal, putting down their napkins. CAMERA comes to rest on

SCENE 29—MEDIUM CLOSE SHOT. A Young Woman, pale and thin, sits before her untouched meal. There is a faraway look in her large eyes.

CUT TO

SCENE 30–MEDIUM LONG SHOT. DINING ROOM. All rise from
table and leave the room. At the same time two
Negro servants, a man and a woman, enter and
begin to clear table. CAMERA moves in to show.

SCENE 31–MEDIUM SHOT. Two Servants, the man by the
empty place, the woman directly opposite by the
untouched place.

CUT TO

SCENE 32–CLOSE SHOT. The Woman as she clears the place
where the food has been left untouched.

WOMAN SERVANT
*Ah declares, if Mrs. Frémont don' take
nourishment she gonna die.*

CUT TO

SCENE 33–CLOSE SHOT. The Man as he clears the place where
nobody sat.

MAN SERVANT
*It's three months now we been settin'
a place fuh Lieutenant Frémont eb-
bery meal, an' he ain't gonna come
back nebber.*

CUT TO

SCENE 34–CLOSE SHOT. The Woman picking up dishes.

WOMAN SERVANT
How you know dat? Mrs. Frémont she

say she know he comin' back. He come
back befoh, she say, an' he come back
dis time, too.

CUT TO

SCENE 35–CLOSE SHOT. The Man picking up dishes.

MAN SERVANT

But dis time he go fudder. Ebbery-
body say he ain't comin' back nebber.
He dead in de deep snow way up in
dem mountains out West.

DISSOLVE TO

SCENE 36–MEDIUM SHOT INTERIOR. MRS. FRÉMONT is pensively pacing her bedroom in nightgown and wrapper. She stops before a dresser, regards her wan face in the mirror, picks up a miniature portrait which stands in a silver frame. She studies it closely.

CUT TO

SCENE 37–CLOSE SHOT of miniature. It is a portrait of Frémont.

DISSOLVE TO

SCENE 38–CLOSE SHOT. FRÉMONT himself. Unlike the portrait, his face is tired, haggard, and bearded. CAMERA moves slowly back to show

SCENE 39–MEDIUM SHOT EXTERIOR. DECK OF A RIVER STEAMBOAT. FRÉMONT is standing at the rail. It is evening. He is wearing a stained and rumpled uniform. He peers ahead into the gloom, paces the deck impatiently, returns to the rail to peer again.

CUT TO

SCENE 40–LONG SHOT EXTERIOR. CAMERA looks over the bow of the steamboat, across the dark water. A few lights twinkle in the distance as the St. Louis levee comes into sight. Eight bells ring midnight somewhere in the steamboat.

CUT TO

SCENE 41–MEDIUM LONG SHOT EXTERIOR. STEAMBOAT making her landing. A rope, thrown from the levee, splashes into the river. Bells jangle. Steam roars from the escape valves.

CUT TO

SCENE 42–CLOSE SHOT. Plunging paddle wheel backing water.

CUT TO

SCENE 43–MEDIUM SHOT. DECK. FRÉMONT waits impatiently for gangplank to go down. As it does he is the first ashore.

CUT TO

SCENE 44–MEDIUM CLOSE SHOT EXTERIOR. FRÉMONT, alone and afoot, is hurrying through the dark, deserted streets of the city's business district.

CUT TO

SCENE 45–MEDIUM LONG SHOT EXTERIOR. FRÉMONT is ap-

proaching a large darkened mansion. He stops
before it and looks up.

CUT TO

SCENE 46–MEDIUM SHOT EXTERIOR. A closed front door.
CAMERA pans from door to windows, showing
one darkened window after another. It swings
from the façade of the mansion to an adjacent
carriage house and comes to rest on a second-
story window, which is open.

CUT TO

SCENE 47–CLOSE SHOT. FRÉMONT picks up a handful of
pebbles and throws them up at the open window.

CUT TO

SCENE 48–CLOSE SHOT EXTERIOR. WINDOW. The face of a
white-haired Negro man peers sleepily out. As
he hears Frémont's voice his eyes grow large and
the whites shine in the dark.

FRÉMONT'S VOICE
(in a loud whisper from below)
Is that you, Gabriel? This is Lieuten-
ant Frémont. Is everybody well? Is
the family all well?

CUT TO

SCENE 49–MEDIUM SHOT. FRÉMONT as seen by Gabriel looking down from the window. He is a shadowy,
foreshortened figure.

GABRIEL'S VOICE
(falteringly)

*Y-yas suh, dey's well, suh. Is dat really
you, Mistuh Frémon'? You ain't a
ghos' come to ha'nt us, is you?*

CUT TO

SCENE 50—CLOSE SHOT. FRÉMONT. He is broadly smiling.

FRÉMONT

*It's really I, Gabriel. I'm home again.
Can you let me into the house without
waking them up?*

CUT TO

SCENE 51—CLOSE SHOT. GABRIEL's head in the open window.

GABRIEL
(all in a rush)

*Yas suh, I can let you in. But Mrs. Fré-
mon', she ain't home. She's at her
cousin's, Miss Anne's, for the night because Mr. Potts he took sick an'* . . .

CUT TO

SCENE 52—MEDIUM SHOT. FRÉMONT. He turns away while the
Negro is still talking and hurries again through
the dark city streets. CAMERA follows him as he
approaches a church, turns in at the parsonage
next door, raises a hand to knock for admittance,
then checks himself and slowly turns back to the

street. He looks over his shoulder at the darkened building and then up at the sky. He moves reluctantly away.

CUT TO

SCENE 53–LONG SHOT. SKY. The first sign of dawn glimmers behind silhouetted chimneys and rooftops.

CUT TO

SCENE 54–MEDIUM SHOT. FRÉMONT walks the streets. He comes to a little park in front of Barnum's Hotel and wearily seats himself on a bench. In the background a night clerk looks out the door, comes forward to stand beside him. He looks closely at the lieutenant and recognizes him.

CLERK

Why, it's Lieutenant Frémont! Great guns, sir, what're you doing out here in the street? You look exhausted. Come in to the hotel. Come in and rest.

FRÉMONT

Thank you, no. I'll just sit here a little while. It was too late—or too early— to wake my family, so I . . .

CLERK

But you might as well be comfortable while you're waiting, sir. You must

need rest. Do come in and lie down
until it gets light.

THE LIEUTENANT, with a wry grin, wearily rises
and follows the clerk into the hotel.

DISSOLVE TO

SCENE 55—MEDIUM SHOT EXTERIOR. VERANDA. The Benton
mansion. In the bright light of morning the entire household, the servants, and a number of
neighbors are gathered. They are chattering excitedly. Old Gabriel is the center of attention.

GABRIEL

Ah tells you Ah saw him plain as Ah
can see you—or you. An' Ah talked
wib him, too.

OLD NURSE

(holding the Frémont baby)
You saw a ghos', tha's what you saw.
Oh Lawdy . . . (she moans)

GABRIEL

Ah don' know if he was a ghos' or not,
but he t'rew pebbles in de window an'
woke me up. An' den he stood dere an'
talked to me plain as Ah'm talkin' now.

CUT TO

SCENE 56—MEDIUM SHOT. A CARRIAGE. It stops in front of the

house. Mrs. Frémont gets out and joins the group
on the veranda. She takes the baby from the
nurse and stands near the front door. Gabriel
steps over to her, and she listens to him.

GABRIEL

*It was de lieutenant Ah saw, Mrs.
Frémont. He woke me up in de middle
ob de night. Ah tole him you was at
Miss Anne's an' he went away as sudden as he come.*

DISSOLVE TO

SCENE 57–MEDIUM SHOT EXTERIOR. FRÉMONT looks somewhat rested but is still in the same disheveled
uniform. He is trying to hurry along the street,
but at every step of the way somebody stops him
to shake his hand, clap him on the back, try to
engage him in conversation. CAMERA follows him
as he makes his way in the direction of the Benton house in company with a growing throng of
enthusiastic welcomers and well-wishers.

VOICES

It's Lieutenant Frémont!

ANOTHER VOICE

Welcome back, son.

ANOTHER VOICE

It's mighty good to see you, John.

ANOTHER VOICE

Hurrah for Lieutenant Frémont!

CUT TO

SCENE 58—MEDIUM SHOT EXTERIOR. FRÉMONT in front of the
Benton house. CAMERA follows him as he breaks
away from the people around him and strides to
the veranda. His wife appears in the doorway.
Oblivious of the crowd around them they plunge
into each other's arms.

DISSOLVE TO

SCENE 59—MEDIUM SHOT EXTERIOR. A STEAMBOAT is tying up
at the levee. A brief SHOT of a busy, noisy scene.

MAN ON STEAMBOAT DECK
(shouting toward the levee)
What's the latest news?

MAN ON LEVEE

Frémont's back!

DISSOLVE TO

SCENE 60—LONG SHOT EXTERIOR. A CITY STREET. It is night.
Torchlight parade. Frémont and his wife ride in
a carriage. Crowds cheer.

DISSOLVE TO

SCENE 61—CLOSE SHOT EXTERIOR. LIEUTENANT AND MRS. FRÉ-
MONT, elegantly dressed for traveling, bid farewell to relatives and friends in front of a steamboat's gangplank.

VOICE

Good-by, Jessie. Good-by, John.

ANOTHER VOICE

Remember us to everyone back in Washington.

ANOTHER VOICE

Give my regards to Senator Benton.

Waving and smiling, the lieutenant and his wife move up the gangplank.

DISSOLVE TO

SCENE 62—LONG SHOT EXTERIOR. STEAMBOAT churns its way up the broad Ohio River.

DISSOLVE TO

SCENE 63—MEDIUM SHOT EXTERIOR. The travel-marked Frémonts, in a carriage, enter Washington, the White House in the background as they ride along the street.

DISSOLVE TO

SCENE 64—MEDIUM SHOT INTERIOR. LIVING ROOM of the Benton house in Washington. It is evening. Senator Benton, and Lieutenant and Mrs. Frémont are seated talking.

FRÉMONT

It's good to be back in Washington. And it's going to be good to get to

*work again now that the worst of the
homecoming is over. There's a lot to
be done—calculations, maps . . .*

SENATOR BENTON

*And you must write your report to
Congress as soon as possible.*

MRS. FRÉMONT

*Yes, John, we must get to work on
your report right away.*

DISSOLVE TO

SCENE 65–LONG SHOT EXTERIOR. STREET SCENE in the bustling frontier town of Independence, Missouri. In the foreground a covered wagon crosses in front of CAMERA. Beyond is a busy blacksmith shop. A large group of men with horses, mules, and oxen mill about in front of the wide doorway. Men and women pick their way through muddy streets.

FRÉMONT'S VOICE

*I wish there were some way you could
have been with me, Jessie. And I wish
you could have been with me too,
Senator, to see that great Western
country in which you are so interested.
It would have done your heart good
to see the wagon trains moving along
the Santa Fe Trail in the spring, last*

*year, and out across the great plains
and over the mountains on the Oregon
Trail. Nearly a thousand people left
the frontier for the Far West last year.*

CUT TO

SCENE 66–LONG SHOT EXTERIOR. COVERED WAGONS head
West, fanning over the flat prairie outside Independence.

SENATOR BENTON'S VOICE
*Yes, and next year, after your maps
and report are published, there'll be
even more, a great many more.*

CUT TO

SCENE 67–MEDIUM SHOT EXTERIOR. FRÉMONT and his men
overtake an emigrant caravan in the South Pass
of the Rocky Mountains. Friendly exchange of
greetings, and then the men on horseback leave
the wagons behind.

FRÉMONT'S VOICE
*It's a vast and wonderful land. After
we crossed the Great South Pass
we went down the Bear River and
through a country of striking scenery
to the Inland Sea, where we remained
and explored until the early signs of
oncoming winter sent us on our way
to Oregon.*

CUT TO

SCENE 68–LONG SHOT EXTERIOR. FRÉMONT'S party, against magnificent mountain scenery, skirts the waters of Great Salt Lake.

DISSOLVE TO

SCENE 69–MEDIUM SHOT EXTERIOR. FRÉMONT'S EXPEDITION pushes through wild terrain in the face of a cold wind and early snow flurries.

FRÉMONT'S VOICE

But the most glorious hour was yet to come. When we got to Oregon I took Kit Carson and two dozen of my best men and headed south into the Great Basin. There, after numerous adventures, I was at last forced by a serious shortage of supplies and equipment to decide to cross into California, which lay only a few miles distant but on the far side of the towering, snowbound Sierra Nevadas. . . .

As Frémont's voice narrates, CAMERA cuts to

SCENE 70–LONG SHOT EXTERIOR. EXPLORER and his party move in an extenuated line along the base of the jagged, white-topped mountains. Slowly the line begins to wind upward, while the voice continues:

. . . They said nobody could cross

that wall in winter. Even the Indians
refused to show us the way.

CUT TO

SCENE 71—MEDIUM CLOSE SHOT EXTERIOR. FRÉMONT by a
campfire in the snow. An old Indian stands beside him, haranguing and gesticulating in the
firelight, telling the white man that it is impossible to get across.

FRÉMONT'S VOICE
. . . *But we did it.*

CUT TO

SCENE 72—MEDIUM SHOT EXTERIOR. MEN AND HORSES floun-
der through deep snow, fighting their way up
the steep mountain. A fierce and desolate scene.
. . . *We crossed the Sierras in the*
dead of winter.

CUT TO

SCENE 73—MEDIUM SHOT EXTERIOR. A GROUP of exhausted
men stand in a high pass, looking down into
California. With the strength born of new hope
they begin the descent down into the green valley as the voice of the narrator continues:
. . . *We descended the western slopes*
into California, where we were hospi-
tably received by Mr. Sutter, who
owns considerable lands in that do-
main.

XIII. Ready for a Fight

Joshua's first visit to the studio was only enough to whet his appetite. When Tex saw how happily Josh was able to keep himself occupied around the lot and that his enthusiasm was not merely a result of fleeting curiosity, he was only too glad to take the boy along to the studio every morning. The arrangement proved beneficial to them both. His nephew's fresh enthusiasm was encouraging to the director at a time when his work was not going smoothly, while Joshua's lessons in movie-making gained emphasis from these same difficulties.

Not that Tex's troubles with the front office, or his own

desire to understand all that was going on, could detract from Joshua's enjoyment of the spectacle of a moving-picture studio at work. There might be difficult moments, but as far as he was concerned there could be no dull ones. If he were not on the set watching rehearsals and takes, he was out to observe the variety of activity that made these sixty walled-in acres such a carnival of wonders.

An entire afternoon could slip by, time unnoticed, while he explored the back lot, where the permanent sets were located. Here, in a sort of great back yard, apart from the sound stages and buildings and traffic, he came upon a Western town. The Last Chance Hotel, the Wells Fargo Bank, saloons, stores, and wooden house fronts faced onto a wide dirt street. Wheel tracks in the dust, hitching-rails along the rough board sidewalk, signs and posters, gave evidence of genuine habitation. But the place was as silent and deserted as a graveyard at midnight; if it were not for the bright daylight and reassuring sounds of nearby hammering it would have been almost as frightening. It seemed that the swinging doors of the Red Dog Saloon must surely burst open to reveal a pistol-toting cowboy in chaps and sombrero, or that the fair face of the schoolmarm from the East must appear at a window of Ma Barker's Boarding House. But Joshua had the town quite to himself. He walked the middle of the street, marveling at the realism of every detail. It was not until he had put it all behind him and then turned back to look from a little distance that the illusion was destroyed and he could see both the false fronts and the frameworks of bare lumber behind them.

Nearby was another street scene—a crooked, cobbled byway of an Old-World village. A curtain fluttered from an open window, and Joshua passed on uneasily. It seemed like the sort of a place where you might stumble on a body, or be confronted by a hooded assassin.

A few steps farther, and he found himself among barrels and crates on a waterfront wharf. The rust-streaked side of a tramp ship loomed over him. He could see the heads of the wooden rivets that held her simulated plates together. Booms and cables stood against the bright sky ready to lift a cargo from the wharf and lower it through her hatchways.

Further exploration revealed a medieval castle and a

tropic lagoon. Stepping from one place to another was like traveling around the world in seven-league boots. It was a completely deserted world, and when he got used to its eeriness he enjoyed having it to himself for a little while. He wandered through it, imagining heroic deeds to go with each marvelous setting, until it occurred to him that the day was over and Tex would soon be ready to leave.

At quitting time Joshua would locate his uncle and stand by to drive home with him as soon as he was ready to go. Sometimes Tex was delayed by a conference, or a look at some rushes of the morning's shooting, and it would be seven or eight o'clock before they got away. Even then the day's work was seldom over, for the busy director, tired but preoccupied with his ideas and problems, would often talk about them during the evening, or begin to think about and plan the next day's work. As Joshua became familiar with all that was going on at the studio, he found himself being taken more and more into his uncle's confidence. The evening discussions became a regular feature to which they both looked forward.

But there was one thing that troubled Joshua. It was not difficult to see that relations between the director and the producer were becoming badly strained, that Tex was, without fully realizing it perhaps, building up a bitter resentment against the man who he felt was standing in the way of his high standards. It was a clash of ideas and personalities, resulting from overwork and fatigue as much as anything else. The situation distressed the boy because it was making his uncle cross and unhappy and because he could see that every day it was growing worse.

One night at the studio Joshua waited for nearly an hour in the car, where it had been agreed that he would meet Tex after work. When the director did not come he grew impatient and went to look for him. He made the rounds of all the customary places where he could expect to find him, but without success. At last some late departer, seeing the boy wandering around by himself, informed him that he would probably find the director in Mr. Beckett's office. It was the only place he had not thought to look.

Entering the administration building, Joshua found the halls deserted. As he approached the producer's office, however, he heard the muffled sounds of voices within, and suddenly it occurred to him that they were shouting. He opened the door timidly to observe a scene that struck him with dismay. There were two grown and ordinarily dignified men, his uncle and Mr. Beckett, with red faces and blazing eyes, facing each other across the desk like two dogs over a bone. Never had he seen his good-natured uncle lose his temper, nor would he have imagined that mild-mannered Mr. Beckett could be transformed into such a formidable figure.

They were so absorbed in their mutual fury that they were unaware of the presence of a third person in the room. Joshua stood frozen in the doorway, not knowing for an interminable minute what to do. They had reached the point where both were too angry to speak. They just stood there, facing each other, and it was plain to see that they were on the verge of blows.

Then, without consciously thinking out what he was doing, Joshua crossed the room and, placing himself between them, grasped his uncle's arm in both his hands. "Let's go home," he heard his own voice say. To his surprise Tex, without taking his eyes off the producer, gave ground and allowed himself to be propelled to the door. Mr. Beckett came from behind the desk and stalked to the center of the room, where he stood glaring after them as Joshua opened the door and stepped out into the hallway, one hand still clutching his uncle's sleeve. Only when the door slammed behind his back did Tex seem to come to his senses and realize where he was and what was happening. He gave the lapels of his coat a fierce yank, turned on his heel, and strode from the building. Joshua followed after him.

They went to the car and got in. In his fury Tex drove like a dare-devil stunt man. Joshua, sitting stiff and scared beside him, held on tightly and hoped that they would be arrested before they crashed. They sped past red lights and wove in and out of traffic at seventy miles an hour. But by some miracle they escaped both the police and an accident. By the time they reached home the director seemed to have spent the worst of his violence. He became himself again, fatigued, sagging, and still silent, but at least the rational man whom Joshua always admired, no matter how extreme his passing mood might be.

After dinner the storm had completely passed. Tex was

ready to talk with his nephew as was their custom. Getting right to the point, he began by trying to offer an explanation for his fight with the producer. But Joshua had seen this coming, and as he looked back he realized that aside from its violence the fight had not really been a surprise to him.

"We've disagreed often enough before," his uncle said, "but we've never fought. I hardly know whose fault it is. Both of ours, I suppose. At any rate, the only thing that keeps me from chucking the whole job is that the picture is so nearly finished. We're going on location next week, and when that's over I hope I'll be able to wash my hands of the whole business."

It was the first mention Joshua had heard of going on location. In spite of the troubled situation he could not help wondering whether he would be able to go too. But this was certainly not the time to try to find out. Tex, his composure regained, had sunk into a big chair in the living room. He wanted to talk. This was the proper occasion for lending a sympathetic ear.

"I suppose it's been brewing a long time," he continued, unable to get the unpleasant episode off his mind. "It's this sequence we're supposed to do at Sacramento that brought it to a head."

"What sequence is that?" asked Joshua, seizing the opportunity to learn about the forthcoming location trip and, at the same time, to lead the conversation away from the recent row.

"We're going up to Northern California to take some scenes at Sutter's Fort. Frémont was there on his third Western expedition."

Joshua quickly reviewed what he had recently managed to choke down of *Go West*. "I guess I haven't gotten that far yet," he had to admit.

"How far have you gotten?" his uncle asked.

"To Frémont's second expedition, when he crossed the Sierras in winter and first came to California."

"Well, you'll find that on his third expedition he came to California again. It was the year 1846, a time of change and unrest around this section. The United States was beginning really to move westward on its last big push across the continent. We were about to go to war with Mexico over Texas and we were on ticklish terms with England as to who owned the Oregon country. When Frémont came to California with a band of straight-shooting mountain men the local governor began to feel uneasy. What were the Americans up to? The more he thought about it the less he liked it. So finally he ordered them to get out. But Frémont wanted to stick around. If there was going to be a war with Mexico, then the province of California, with all the American settlers who had been moving in lately and making homes, was a ripe plum ready to fall. He wanted to be around to pick it up for Uncle Sam before England could get it."

"Gosh," said Joshua, "it gets sort of complicated."

"That's just it," Tex agreed. "It gets so complicated that

when you try to make it into a picture you're apt to get a lot of people standing around talking and explaining things until it's about as exciting as watching a chess game. But I think it's possible to film it in an exciting way. You'd have to imagine that you were really there, that you didn't know what was going to happen next. If you were an American who had settled out here you'd be wondering how you were going to be able to keep from losing your home. You'd be wondering if there really was going to be a war. Everything would be a question to which you didn't know the answer. If I could get Beckett to realize that there was plenty of action and suspense going on and that we don't have to run in any maudlin fiction in order to get a good story! But no. He's convinced that history and the box office don't go together, and so I have to turn out something that I hate to have my name associated with."

Joshua had thought that they were getting away from the subject of the producer for a little while, but now as Tex mentioned his name his voice got tense and angry. In an attempt to bring the conversation back to the safe ground of history Joshua quickly asked, "What happened? What did Frémont do when the governor ordered him out?"

"Frémont?" said Tex, having to think twice before he could pick up the thread of the conversation. "Oh, yes. Well, he acted sort of as if he knew that some day he was going to be the hero of a moving picture. His big trouble, though, was the same as mine—the script was no good."

"What d'you mean?"

"He was playing the part of a man of action, you see, a regular movie hero. But suddenly he found himself in a scene that was complicated and unclear. So, instead of having a hero who simply sees his duty and does it, we have one who can't make up his mind. He is ordered out of the country. It is an insult to the American flag. So he defies the Mexican governor. He takes up a position on a hilltop and gets ready for a fight. Well, that's great stuff; the public always loves it. But then there isn't any fight after all. He changes his mind, and after a few days he and his men pull out and head up north toward Oregon. They move slowly because the hero still hopes that the script will be changed and will call for him to rush back and fight the Mexicans and win a new territory for his country. Before many days have passed he changes his mind again. He decides to try tinkering with the script himself. So he turns around and heads back toward Sutter's Fort. He makes camp a few miles away, and it begins to look as if something interesting might happen."

At this point Tex got to his feet and began thoughtfully to pace the room. "It's right here that I've got to get some changes in the script," he said. "It's here that I know I have to simplify and dramatize the situation. You see, the Mexican government has sent messengers to the Indians telling them to get on the warpath and make life miserable for the American settlers and maybe they'll get discouraged and go back where they came from. This gives Frémont a

chance to do something. He rides against the Indian villages and scatters the war parties before they even get
started. There's not much to it. But the settlers rally around
Frémont. They want action as much as he does. A bunch of
them ride up to Sonoma and take a Mexican general pris-
oner. Then they declare Northern California an independent republic. Well, it really wasn't, of course. But the
important thing, as I see it, is that this was an hour of crisis.
The future course of local history hung in balance. That's
the idea I want to get on film."

He continued to pace up and down, and Joshua waited
for him to go on. But after a minute's silence Tex gave his
head a shake, as though to get the matter out of his mind.
He went back to his chair. "Well," he said, "you'll be able
to see better for yourself what I'm driving at when we get
up there on location and take these scenes around the fort."

"When are we going?" asked Joshua, pleased with the
answer to the unasked question that was uppermost in his
mind.

"If you'd like to come, then you and I are going to drive
up this Sunday," said his uncle. "Some of the technicians
are going up ahead, but the whole crew won't get there until sometime Monday." He heaved a great sigh. "Believe me,
it's going to be good to get away from the studio and work
in peace for a few days."

"Gosh," said Joshua, "history or moving pictures, the
more a fellow learns the more there is to learn."

"You can say that again," agreed Tex.

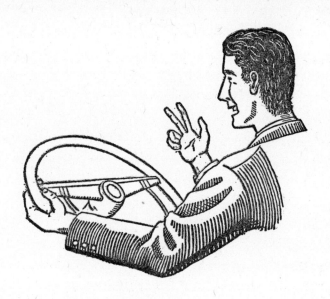

XIV. Sutter's Fort

By driving to Sacramento on a Sunday Tex and Joshua were able to make something of a holiday of the four-hundred-mile trip up through Central California via the broad San Joaquin Valley.

They got off to an early morning start. The weather was warm and bright. Tex was so happy to be leaving the studio and its recent aggravations behind that he behaved like a schoolboy on the first day of vacation. He bellowed snatches of songs, made silly jokes, and laughed from sheer exuberance. Speeding smoothly northward with the top of the car down and the wind in their faces, they both forgot for a few hours that there was a care in the world.

As the day and the miles slipped by Joshua was able to get a wide and comprehensive view of hundreds of miles of the state's varied terrain. On the right, far across the valley floor, rose the peaks of the Sierra Nevadas, the towering wall across which the pioneer immigrant bands had struggled, often in a life-and-death race against the treacherous early snows of autumn. The distant mountain range ran parallel to the valley so that for hours the picture remained much the same; only the foreground of cultivated fields and expansive orchards, ranch houses and roadside buildings, changed with the passing miles. On the left, to the west, more irregular and less lofty than the splendid Sierra Nevadas, ran the coastal ranges that edged the Pacific. High mountains, broad valleys, and a shore of the greatest of oceans joined to form a single geographic unit—the golden state of California. It was unlike any country Joshua had ever seen before, and he liked it.

Sacramento, the state capital, is situated on the upper reaches of the central valley, about seventy miles northeast of San Francisco. It being Sunday, the city streets were quiet and almost empty, but at the hotel where Joshua and his uncle were expected they found a livelier scene. In the lobby, coming and going, were a good many of the men who had preceded them from the studio. Bud Shore, the cameraman, came forward to greet them and launched into a report on the preliminary accomplishments that had occupied him since his arrival.

Joshua followed the talking men to the hotel desk where

Tex registered in the book which the clerk placed in front of him. The boy watched his uncle sign his name, then took the pen and signed his own. As he blotted the wet ink his eye ran over the other names on the page and was suddenly arrested by the signature of Mr. Robert Beckett. In his surprise he interrupted the conversation of the director and camerman without looking up from the book. "Hey, Tex," he abruptly exclaimed, "I thought you said that Mr. Beckett wasn't going to be here."

"That's right," Tex said with a startled look, "I did."

Joshua pointed to the signature in the registry book.

"Yeah," said the cameraman. "I didn't expect to see him up here either. But he came yesterday. I haven't talked to him, but he's been snooping around the set and keeping an eye on everything we're doing. What's come over him anyway?"

"He doesn't want to let me out of his sight!" Tex exploded. "That's what's come over him. He's got the idea in his head that I'm not going to do these scenes up here the way he wants them."

Bud Shore looked surprised at the vehemence with which Tex spoke. But Joshua realized what a letdown it was for his uncle to learn that he was not escaping, after all, the tension and quarreling which had made his recent weeks at the studio so difficult. On the way up he had been in high spirits because he was getting away and because he was looking forward to being able to finish the job in peace. It had seemed almost as good as a vacation—and here it turned out that the very thing he was trying to escape had preceded him in the person of Mr. Beckett.

But after his initial outburst Tex said no more about it. He fell into that quiet, thoughtful mood that had become familiar to Joshua of late. The cameraman, apparently unaware of how bad was the conflict between the director and the producer, cheerfully suggested that they have dinner and led the way to the dining room. During the meal he did most of the talking. When it was finished Tex arose from the table and announced that while it was still daylight he was going over to the fort to take a look around.

"If you don't mind I won't go with you," said the cameraman. "I'll see enough of that place during working hours. I told some of the boys I'd go to the movies with 'em tonight."

Joshua could not help laughing. Bud Shore looked at him with a smile. "It sounds like a busman's holiday, I suppose. But after all, it's not often that I get a chance to sit back and relax and *enjoy* a picture."

Joshua went with his uncle to look at the famous fort which was to be their set. It occupied a level green area within the city's limits. From outside it was a ten- or twelve-foot wall in a park-like area surrounded by paved streets and close-packed buildings. There was just enough open ground around it to make it possible to ignore for a moment the incongruous surroundings and picture what the local scene might have been like a hundred years ago.

As they approached the gate Tex explained to Joshua that this was a reconstruction of the original fort, which had been the headquarters of an estate so large that it almost amounted to a private domain. From here John Sutter, who was a Swiss immigrant, had directed his numerous affairs. He had employed Indians to work in the fields and at the numerous domestic tasks that such a huge establishment demanded. He had even kept a private army of Indians in uniform who drilled and marched in front of the fort. Indian and Mexican cowboys, called *vaqueros*, had tended the herds of horses and cattle. American travelers, newly arrived in California, usually made this their first stopping place. If any of them were in need of jobs, friendly Captain Sutter could always manage to find work for them.

The babble of many tongues, the whinnying and the

stamping of horses, the clang of the blacksmith's hammer—
all the onetime frontier symphony was long since stilled.
The clamor and the color had faded away, but the façade
of the place was still much as it had been in those days.
Entering the big gate, which was flanked by two tall palm
trees, Joshua could see that the thick adobe walls enclosed
a rectangular space about a hundred yards long. In the
center loomed a two-story adobe building, and all around,
against the outer wall, stood numerous low structures,
which apparently housed living quarters, workrooms, and
stables.

The fort was now a historical museum posted with numerous little signs to explain how each room and each piece
of equipment had once been used. Many relics of old California, from hunting knives to freight wagons, were on dis-
play. In the failing light it was getting hard to see, and
Joshua put off a complete investigation of the premises for
the next day.

This evening he followed Tex around while the director
looked over the preparatory work that had been done by
carpenters and electricians and began making his own
preliminary estimates of camera angles and compositions.
With occasional comments made half to himself and half
aloud he squatted to study an imaginary shot from close
to the ground or moved thoughtfully from place to place,
holding his hands outstretched before his face to frame an
imaginary scene. "Kit Carson and Frémont come galloping
through the open gate," he mumbled. "Indians lounging

in the foreground. Sutter steps out of that doorway and crosses from right to left. Hmm, that might work out all right."

Joshua stood behind him, watching him work, as though he were looking over the shoulder of an artist as he sketched a landscape. It was a landscape with a deep perspective that went back into time as well as space. It was magic, as a matter of fact, that the director was brewing, a miraculous spell which could bring back to life the scenes and people of a hundred years ago.

As Tex, closely followed by Joshua, moved about the silent and deserted fort, visualizing and reconstructing bits of its past, an apparition suddenly stood before their startled eyes. It seemed to be a materialization of the director's imaginings, if not a solid product of his magic. The gigantic figure of a man wearing a long fringed hunting shirt loomed in the gateway. In their surprise they both gave ground uneasily. But then they stopped, the director because of common sense, and Joshua because he recognized the apparition. It was the towering person of Jedediah Meade.

He stood there for a few seconds, looking around, taking in what he could see of the fort's interior in the twilight. His glance included the man and the boy who were silently gaping at him. With a casual "Howdy" he stepped toward them.

"It—it's Jedediah Meade," Joshua at last managed to say.

Upon hearing the boy's voice the old man recognized his friend at once. "Why, howdy, boy," he said with warm surprise. "What in thunder're you doin' in these parts?"

"This is my uncle," said Joshua. "I came up with him."

Tex shook the giant's outstretched hand. "We're here to do some work on the picture," he said. "What're *you* doing here? Josh told me you'd gone back to Kansas."

"I'm on my way. This old coon travels kinda slow. Not so young as I once were. I been takin' it kinda easy and lookin' round the country. I just thought I'd like to take a look at the old fort while I was near by." He paused to turn his head this way and that and peer into the gloom, almost as though he were looking for something. But it was getting so dark that only dim forms were visible, and the top of the wall against the pale sky. Then, "Say," he said, "how's the pitcher comin'?"

The director's only answer was a shake of the head. Joshua interrupted the silence which followed by explaining, "It's almost finished. But Tex doesn't think it's too good."

"What's the trouble?" asked the old man.

"Oh, that's a long story," Tex said curtly, as though he wanted to dismiss the subject. But then he regarded Meade thoughtfully and seemed to change his mind. "No, I'll tell you what's wrong with it," he said. "It's a picture that's supposed to be about what really happened here a hundred years ago. But it's being turned into a lot of sloppy fiction —not good fiction, but sloppy fiction. And d'you know why? Because they think their sentimental fiction is more exciting than history."

"Well, mebbe that's true of some history," said Meade. "There's a heap of things I don't know. But I do know it ain't true about Californy and Sutter's Fort. I can tell 'ee that."

"Exactly," said Tex. "But try to prove it to a mule-headed producer."

"I don't know nothin' about producers neither. But there's been fightin' an' bleedin' and dyin' around these parts, an' action enough fer a barrel of movin' pitchers—a heap more than the history books can tell 'ee."

"More than the history books can tell you?" Tex repeated with interest. "What makes you say that?"

" 'Cause nobody rightly knows the whole story, least-wise nobody who was never there." The old man rubbed his chin and frowned reflectively.

"Oh, I think that the whole story is known," said Tex. "There's certainly been enough written about it. It's just that when we look back at the past we take everything for granted and don't realize how much suspense and action and how many close calls accompanied all those events while they were happening. We know that at the time of the Mexican War the relationship between the Mexican politicos and the American settlers in California was pretty badly strained. But we don't stop to think of just what it must have been like to have made the long journey out here from the States and settled down and then found

yourself in danger of losing the home which you had come to consider your own. We know that the Mexicans tried to take the land away from the American settlers and tried to get the Indians to go on the warpath against them, but we don't stop to think of—"

"That's it!" Jedediah Meade interrupted. "That's what I been tryin' to remember."

"What?" Tex asked in surprise.

"The time Frémont busted up them Injun war parties. That was the prettiest fight 'ee ever hope to hear tell of."

"Why, there wasn't much of a fight," said Tex. "Frémont and his men rode into the villages and scattered the Indians before they ever had a chance to get going."

"Oh, there was a fight," insisted Meade. "It's just like I told 'ee. The history books don't know it all."

"I suppose that's so," said the director, contemplating the huge man thoughtfully. Joshua, standing by and glancing from one to the other, could see that his uncle's curiosity was aroused. He was interested in Meade and more than willing to hear his story.

But the old man seemed quite oblivious of the fact that he had won a sympathetic ear. Looking up at the sky, he seemed to dismiss entirely the subject under discussion with the abrupt remark, "It's gettin' dark. This old coon better be makin' tracks."

He touched the brim of his hat and was on the point of turning away when Tex reached out a restraining hand and took hold of his sleeve. "What about that fight?" he demanded.

"What fight?" Meade innocently asked.

"Why, the fight when Frémont rode out to put down the Indian—"

"Oh, that one," said the old man. "Scalp my old head, that *was* the prettiest fight. . . ."

XV. The History Books Don't Know It All

"The history books don't know it all," Meade repeated, slowly shaking his head from side to side. "They don't tell 'ee 'bout the five men got separated from Frémont not far from here an' was attacked by a hundred Injuns, do they?"

"I've never heard about it if they do," said Tex.

"But that's what happened. I'll tell 'ee how it came about. There was five of Frémont's men got chasin' off on their own after some Injuns an' were separated from the main party. Well, that was all right. They just figgered they'd take a short cut an' join up with the cap'n a little further on. They was ridin' along across an open stretch of ground when they spotted four or five Injuns on horseback come ridin' over a ridge a little ways off. The white men was just about to light out after 'em when thew saw there was still more of the same behind the ridge, a big party of 'em an'

all mounted. Well, the shoe was on the other foot, as they
say, an' it was either run or fight. There wasn't a tree or a
bush around for cover, an' it 'peared like the Injuns was too
close to get away from an' weren't goin' to get no further.
So they stood their ground."

The old man paused. It had gotten so dark that Joshua
could hardly see his face. But his compelling voice held his
listeners spellbound. "What did they do?" the boy asked
eagerly.

"Well one of Frémont's men jumped to the ground an'
pulled his knife an' cut his horse's throat. Quicker'n 'ee can
say 'rattlesnakes' the rest of 'em did the same. They flung
themselves down behind the kickin' carcasses an' looked to
their rifles. The Injuns came chargin' down on 'em an' two of
the white men fired. They hit the chief who was ridin' at the
head of the attack, an' when he fell the Injuns behind him
split into two columns an' galloped by on either side,
shootin' their arrows into the dead horses until they looked
like porcupines. As quick as they had rode by they wheeled

around an' charged again. This time the other three men fired an' brought down two more Injuns. But when they wheeled an' charged again none of Frémont's men had had time to reload. It looked like the end, all right."

"But it wasn't, was it?" breathed Joshua.

Jedediah Meade did not answer right away, and into the brief silence there plunged a new voice. "Go on, what happened?" it demanded.

The director, the old giant, and the boy looked sharply around to discover a man standing beside them. He had approached unnoticed in the dark, and as he stepped close Joshua recognized Mr. Beckett.

"Go on," the producer said to the old man, ignoring Tex and Joshua. "Finish your story."

Meade gazed calmly down on his suddenly enlarged audience. "Well," he said in his deep and vigorous tones, "the Injuns came gallopin' in for the kill. But all of a sudden their horses began to go crazy. They reared an' they bucked an' they threw their riders like it was a rodeo. They had caught the smell of blood from the dead horses, ye see, an' they would go no closer. So Frémont's men were able to load up and hold 'em off until it got dark."

"And then did they all get away?" asked Joshua.

"Yes," said Meade. "Under cover of night they crept away. But one of 'em had a mighty close squeeze. He was

wounded so bad that the others left him for dead. An Injun stumbled on him in the dark an' bent down to take
his hair. But the white man came to an' jumped up an'
killed the Injun an' got away."

"That's quite a story, all right," said Tex. "How d'you
know it really happened?"

"My daddy tole me," said the old man, "an' he was
there."

"Jumping jiminy!" exclaimed Mr. Beckett, now turning excitedly to Tex. "Where did you find this guy? He's
worth a thousand bucks a week."

"He sort of found us," said Tex. "Don't ask me how."

In their enthusiasm both men were acting as though
there never had been a word of disagreement between
them. "Come on," said the producer, "all of you. Let's get
back to the hotel. I've got an idea."

Mr. Beckett ushered Jedediah Meade out to his car and
seated the giant beside him with all the deference that he
would show to a vice-president from the front office or a
visiting banker from New York. Tex and Joshua got into
their car and followed the producer.

"Gee," said the boy when he and his uncle were alone,
"his father was actually there. He was the J. Meade who
Mrs. Horseman has on her list."

"He must have been," agreed Tex.

"D'you s'pose that's true about the Indian fight? D'you
s'pose he really knows things that aren't in the history
books?"

"I don't know, Josh. He's a natural storyteller. No doubt he's telling the truth, but who can say for sure whether it happened just the way he says or not? What does it really matter? The main thing is that he's giving us just what we need—a convincing incident of action. And, what's more, it looks like he's convinced Beckett at the same time, which is what I've been trying to do for weeks."

Back at the hotel the producer hurried them into an elevator and up to the sitting room of his suite on the top floor. Hustling about even more busily than was his customary manner, he offered them chairs and then, without further explanation as to what was on his mind, he picked up the telephone and put through a call to Hollywood.

Joshua, his uncle, and Jedediah Meade, arrayed in a semicircle around the room, could do nothing but sit awkwardly watching and listening as Mr. Beckett got his secretary on the other end of the wire and excitedly instructed her to contact three studio writers, whom he named, and tell them to go to the Los Angeles airport and board a plane which would be waiting. She was to accompany them and make sure that they all got to Sacramento tonight, as soon as possible.

Then he called the Los Angeles airport and after a little trouble succeeded in chartering the plane that was to stand by for the writers.

When he had put down the telephone he began to pace back and forth in the middle of the room with his shoulders hunched, his head thrown back, and his hands in his pockets. "Tex," he said, clearing his throat, "I want to apologize to you."

"That's not neces—" the director began.

"Yes it is," Mr. Beckett insisted. "And furthermore I want to tell you why I came up here. I didn't come to spy on you. It was just that I was worried about our—er, differences of opinion, and about the way this picture's been going. I came up to try to dope out some way we could get together on this job and finish it up right. This evening one of the boys told me you had gotten here and gone over to the fort. So I went right over there to get hold of you."

"If there's any apologizing to be done," said Tex, "I guess I'm the one who should be apologizing for losing my temper."

"Well, it doesn't matter now, as long as we can get together and get on with the show. Mr. Meade here seems to have the answer to our problem, and I don't think we'll have to change the script much to get what we both want, which is plenty of action without departing from the historical point of view. Right?"

"Right," agreed Tex. "What d'you suggest?" Behind the producer's back he winked cheerfully at Joshua.

"I should say that what we've got to do is change this Fort Sutter sequence around so that it shows the whole thing more from the point of view of the American settlers here in California. They're in danger of losing their homes, and some of 'em decide to revolt against the Mexicans. But instead of a lot of talk about independence and the

American flag we'll show how the Indians have been stirred up to go on the warpath against them. Then when Frémont rides out to put down the Indians we'll have a good fight, just like Mr. Meade described it. So long as our history has that kind of action I'll take it, and so will the public. How does that sound to you, Tex?"

Tex weighed the producer's suggestions judiciously. "It sounds pretty good," he slowly said. "But how about our schedule? We've got everybody coming up here tomorrow and we're supposed to get 'em in front of the cameras the next day. We don't have much time for rewriting the script."

"We won't need much time," said Mr. Beckett. "We'll work all night if we have to and get it fixed up by tomorrow. I'll take a copy back with me, and you can go on shooting as scheduled. Do all the background stuff you need around here and we'll take the fight back at the studio."

Tex had picked up a copy of the script while the producer was pacing and talking. He opened it to the place under discussion. "Here," he said, pointing out a line, "is where we'll have to begin making our changes."

Mr. Beckett drew a chair up beside him and sat down. They began to exchange various suggestions. Joshua came and stood quietly behind them to look over their shoulders at the script. Jedediah Meade sat uncomfortably, forgotten for a few minutes, but as the producer and director talked out their ideas he was soon entering into the discussion with a comment here and a suggestion there. His remarks were rough-hewn but to the point. He was, as Tex had said, a natural storyteller. Soon he was supplying most of the material for the revisions.

An hour later Mr. Beckett, his hat on his head as usual, but with his coat now off and his shirtsleeves rolled, got up from his chair to stretch and rest and review their progress. Looking over the rapidly scribbled notes that littered the floor, he said, "What we need is somebody to take this all down properly and keep it in order."

"I could do it," said Joshua. "If you can get me a typewriter I'm pretty good with it."

"Say, that would be great. I don't know why I bothered to send for those writers. I don't think we're even going to need 'em. We'll get Bud Shore up here and have a regular story conference right now." The producer called the cameraman to find out that he was at the movies but would soon be back. Leaving word that he was to come up as soon as possible, Mr. Beckett made several more calls and managed to locate an available typewriter. As soon as it arrived Joshua set himself up at a desk in a corner and was ready to get to work typing the revised dialogue and camera instructions from the notes as they were presented and explained to him.

When Bud Shore made his appearance the session began in earnest. The director, the producer, the cameraman, and Jedediah Meade sat around in a cloud of smoke and talked and argued and scribbled. Now and then the old man would get into a story and the others would listen to him until they heard what they wanted; then they would interrupt him to work on the script and fit his suggestions into place. When a few pages had been roughed out they would be turned over to Joshua for typing.

And so it went, hour after hour, until at last they came to the point where they realized that they were finished. Not only was the job done, but all present were agreed that now it was right. Joshua, as he pulled the last page from the typewriter, looked out the window and saw that the first light of morning was graying the sky. He was tired.

In the untidy sitting room Bud Shore had thrown himself on a sofa and closed his eyes. He was tired too. But Tex and Mr. Beckett were too flushed with triumph to be aware of any ill effects from their night's work. As for Jedediah Meade—well, when they were ready to congratulate him for the important part he had played in saving the situation he was nowhere to be found. Nobody was sure just when he had last been in the room, although they all knew that it was only a little while ago. Perhaps he had just stepped out for a minute or gone downstairs.

At the mention of the word downstairs Mr. Beckett emphatically declared that he was famished. The dining room would soon be open. They would all go down to look for Mr. Meade and then have breakfast. It was a unanimously agreeable suggestion.

As they were getting ready to leave the room they heard the scuffle of feet in the hall and a knock on the door. Mr. Beckett's secretary and the three writers had arrived. They entered looking cold and unhappy and accompanied by enough luggage to get them around the world. The producer greeted them with high-spirited, but nonetheless exaggerated, exuberance. "Glad to see you," he cried. "Glad to see you. It's a shame you didn't get here just a little sooner. I could've introduced you to our up-and-coming new writer. He's sensational, the greatest storyteller in the picture business. Wait'll you meet him."

The writers looked at each other. Bewilderment and something suggestive of disgust mingled on their chilled countenances. "I suppose," said one, "that this is another instance of too little and too late."

"You couldn't have put it better if you'd coined the phrase yourself," said Mr. Beckett. "But now that you're here, make yourselves at home. We're going down to breakfast."

XVI. Appearances and Departures

Jedediah Meade could not be found, although both Joshua and Mr. Beckett spent a large part of the morning in an effort to do so.

The old man had made a strong impression on the producer, who was all for taking him back to the studio. "Why," he proclaimed, "the guy's terrific! What a character! He talks stories like you or I talk about the weather or what we did last night. He'd be a gold mine in Hollywood; and boy, wouldn't he be sensational riding around in a big, long lavender convertible?"

But Mr. Beckett had to forego the personal triumph of bringing his sensational find back with him. That he was disappointed there could be no doubt. But Joshua had a good idea of what Jedediah Meade thought of Hollywood.

He knew there was small chance of getting him to go back even if he could be found in time.

For his own part Joshua was disappointed because he wanted to explain to the old man what a favor he had done for them all. He wanted to thank him, and talk to him some more, and—well, the truth of the matter was that his curiosity was far from satisfied. He wanted to ask him about the father who had explored the Wild West with Frémont and Carson, and about himself: how far back could *he* remember into the history which he talked about in such familiar terms? Who was he, anyway? He clung to the hope that the old man might still show up again, after Mr. Beckett left, or perhaps in the event that things did not go well on the set. He seemed to have a remarkable proclivity for turning up at the moment when his presence could do the most good.

But as it turned out everything did go well on the set. The rest of the location crew arrived and shooting began on schedule. The weather remained good, day after day. Joshua even got into a scene as an extra. By the end of the week the work was successfully completed, and Tex had to admit that maybe the picture was not going to be such a bad one after all.

And so actors, technicians, and equipment were dispatched back to Hollywood, and Joshua and his uncle drove home. They did not have the fine day that they had enjoyed the week before for their return journey, but after what had been so satisfactorily accomplished at Sacramento

they were feeling much too good to be bothered by anything as incidental as the weather.

When, in the evening, they arrived home, it was to find
a delightful surprise: Joshua's mother and father were
there to welcome them. It was a merry reunion. Not only
was the family glad to be together, but each of them had
glowing reports to give the others. Mr. and Mrs. Beacon,
tanned and rested, talked about their leisurely trip through
the Southwest. Tex, happy about his work for the first time
in many days, was able to say that the picture was going
well and was nearing completion. And Joshua, of course,
now held forth on his favorite subject with the full authority of one who had experienced what he was talking about.

Into this pleasant occasion, however, Mr. Beacon at
last introduced a suddenly sobering note. He had recently
received, he explained, a telegram from New York; for
urgent business reasons he was going to have to cut short
his vacation and return home. It was too bad but it could
not be helped. To Joshua especially it came as a hard blow.
He had hoped that he might be able to see the picture
through to the end.

Tex too was disappointed. But after everything had
turned out so well there was nothing to be gained by
mourning over the inevitable. He attempted to console
his nephew by pointing out that he had not only been on
hand to witness the major part of the job, but he had done
more than he probably realized in helping him, as the
director, to see it through. Furthermore, shooting was

going to be completed in another five or six days, and there remained only the cutting and editing.

"But that's just it," Joshua lamented. "Cutting and editing is an important step and I don't like to miss it."

"Yes," said Tex, "it is an important step. But you won't be missing much. You've seen the cutting room and how it's done. And anyway, it's not a thing you can watch very well. It's a creative process of selecting the film that best tells the story, of eliminating all that's unessential and repetitious. It's something you'll learn by doing rather than by watching—and you'll have the chance to do it when you edit your picture that you've been making at school."

In the end Joshua had to admit that he had already been more than fortunate in his Hollywood experience. And there *was* The Movie to begin thinking about once more. He was going to have the opportunity to apply many lessons learned from the top picture makers in the country. The realization made him begin to feel almost eager to get home and back to work on his own enterprise. This was, after all, not the end but the very beginning of his moving-picture career.

It was agreed that the three Beacons would remain one more day in Los Angeles before starting eastward. As Mr. and Mrs. Beacon had driven around the city exploring and sightseeing while Joshua and Tex were in Northern California, they were now interested in making the most of this last chance to pay a visit to the studio. The director, able to spare little time from his work on the first day back from location, had to delegate the job of guide to Joshua, who handled it with an impressive show of knowledge.

During this tour of the lot they stopped by the research department, which was a point of especial interest to Mr. Beacon. Here Joshua encountered Mrs. Horseman. He had not seen her to speak to since the day he had been taken on *his* first tour of the studio. "Oh," she said as soon as she saw him, "I've been thinking of you. I found something on that man Meade whom you were so curious about." She took down a book from the shelf, opened it, and handed it to him.

Joshua read the passages she pointed out. There, in sev-

eral paragraphs, was a brief account of the story Jedediah
Meade had told at Sutter's Fort about the fight between a
hundred Indians and five white men. And one of the lat-
ter was named Meade. He was mentioned as being a very
tall man, and it was he who was wounded and came so near
to losing his scalp.

"It's all I could find about him," said Mrs. Horseman.

"It's plenty," Joshua exclaimed. "May I take it home tonight and show it to my uncle?"

"Surely," she said. "I would've called it to his attention
sooner, but I just found it last week while he was away."

Tex, when he learned that the old man's story was in a
history book after all, was as delighted as Joshua. In looking it over carefully, however, he noticed that the fight
had not taken place during Frémont's attack on the Indian
villages, but at a somewhat earlier time and a different
place.

Joshua's fire was temporarily dampened. But it seemed
to make little difference to Tex. "When Meade told us that
story," he said, "he got Beckett and me together and
helped us out of a bad spot. What does it matter if he
slightly altered a few details of time and place? That's a
storyteller's privilege."

"But you can't tell what to believe and what not to believe," protested Joshua.

"When I hear a story," said Tex, "I care, first, whether it's
good or not, and last whether it's true or not. Even in

history the facts intermingle with the legends. When you're making movies the legends and the tall stories that have grown out of historic incidents can help you to put your point across in an entertaining way and give it life. The thing I object to and want to avoid is the ready-made kind of fiction that makes one picture just like another, instead of like reality. Meade came along in time to give us the touches of authentic flavor we needed."

"He's almost like a ghost," said Joshua, "the way he shows up and disappears, except that he always comes to help, and there's nothing scary about him."

"Yes, but he's genuine enough," Tex said. "When he was a young man, the West was a lot younger. He feels himself closely associated with the early West; his recollections and the stories he heard from his father are just as vivid to him as the present. He's a link between the last frontier and today. In the West you still find a few of 'em around."

Joshua thought this over for a minute. "What d'you s'pose happened to him?" he asked.

"I don't know. He seems to be a pretty independent fellow, likes to go his own way. I guess maybe he went back to Kansas like he said he was going to."

"But it's funny he didn't even say good-by."

"Well, that's his way I guess," said Tex. "I think maybe he was afraid Beckett was going to make him go back to Hollywood and work for the movies."

On their day of departure the Beacons bid Tex an early morning farewell and drove to San Francisco. They had come West over the Santa Fe Trail, and now Joshua's father was interested in following, insofar as time permitted, a route which would approximate the way pioneer settlers had traveled across the Rocky Mountains to California and Oregon.

The second morning of their return journey found them passing through Sacramento, where they stopped to visit Sutter's Fort. Joshua's mother and father, looking around the museum, were pleasantly astounded to discover how much historical knowledge and interest their son had acquired in the past few weeks. He talked of the early days of the fort with such enthusiasm and described so intelligently the problems of making history into moving pictures that a large part of the morning slipped by before Mr. Beacon remembered that he had little time to spare and they must keep moving.

Soon after leaving Sacramento they were in the gradually rising foothills of the Sierras. The conversation turned to the subject of gold, for it was in these wooded hills, where Captain Sutter had sent a party of his men to build a sawmill, that the discovery was made which started the gold rush of 1849.

They saw the stony streams and rivers in which, a hundred years ago, pure gold could be sifted from the sand. Impressed as Joshua was, however, with the thought that

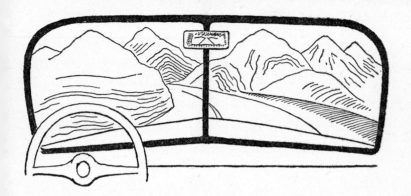

at one time fortunes were to be had here for the taking, he knew that the gold rush had meant the end of old California, and Sutter's empire, and the entire era about which he was excited. It had brought people crowding to the Pacific Coast from the East and from many foreign countries, and although it was a turning point in the history of the place it was a different story from the one that at present filled his fancy.

Over the modern highway, riding in a powerful automobile, the miles that had taken the pioneers hours to cover were disposed of in a matter of minutes. Joshua's imagination clung, as they climbed, to those bands of mountain men, explorers, and settlers—Kit Carson, Lieutenant Frémont, and all the rest—limping down into the green foothills from the terrible heights which, even as he mused, were now looming just ahead. The trees were becoming sparse, the ground rocky and barren. The landscape at the summit was stark and wild, but the spacious view of craggy peaks and up-ended terrain demanded another stop.

Getting out of the car, they were greeted by an immense silence. Joshua was overawed. Close to where he stood, Frémont and his men, and many others after them, had struggled afoot across this sky-high wall. He would have liked to leave the road to explore a little and try his own feet on that rugged ground. But his mother and father were already getting back into the car. There was no use ignoring the hint. Reluctantly he followed them.

The descent of the eastern slopes of the mountains was an abrupt drop down into the arid Nevada waste, the desolate Great Basin that lies between the Sierras and the Rockies. The hurrying Beacons drove for hours without seeing a town or even a house. There were only endless, rock-littered hills, arching their backs against a gray sky, and always in the distance some range of barren desert mountains.

The landscape was monotonous, but its very emptiness enabled them to make good time. Mr. Beacon at last felt justified in relaxing his determined effort and began to show some of his customary interest and curiosity in regard to his surroundings. Not that there was much in this vast scene to claim especial notice, but at one point he slowed down for a spectacular vista of the bald hills, and a little farther along the way he remarked upon a small byroad that left the highway and ran off into the ragged desert. This narrow track that apparently led no place took his fancy and to the surprise of his family he suddenly turned onto it.

APPEARANCES AND DEPARTURES

Neither Joshua nor his mother made any comment. Jouncing and swaying over the stones and ruts was a diversion from the monotony of racing hour after hour over a road that was always the same—perhaps that was the reason they were doing it. At any rate, poking into out of the way corners and side roads was more the sort of thing they were accustomed to.

They proceeded slowly for several miles without discovering anything except that the way got rougher the farther they went. There was still no sign of human habitation anywhere around nor any apparent reason for the road's existence. The afternoon was getting late, and it soon became obvious that there could be no point in continuing farther. Having obeyed his whim and found that there was little to be learned by any such brief excursion as a hurried tourist might take time for, Mr. Beacon stopped the car on a level hilltop and turned it around.

It was at this moment that Joshua pointed out the solitary figure of a man walking across the desolate hills. He was only a small, dark shape in the distance, but he was silhouetted clearly against the sky as he crossed the crest of a rise.

"Now where on earth could he be walking from, or to?" asked Mrs. Beacon. Her husband slowed the car, and they watched him until he moved off the ridge and was almost lost from view. Then they rolled forward again and jounced back the way they had come for about a quarter of a mile before coming to a sudden stop. "Something's

wrong," Mr. Beacon announced. He and Joshua got out to investigate the trouble. The left front tire was flat.

When Joshua opened the rear trunk to get the tools he discovered that the jack was missing. The whole family searched the car, but it was nowhere to be found. "The last time we used it was back in Kansas, when we were coming West," Mr. Beacon ruefully recalled. "I'm afraid we must have forgotten to put it back in the car."

It was a disheartening predicament. Evening was coming on, they were off the highway, and the car could not be moved unless they elected to run for miles over a rough road with a flat tire. "The best thing I can think of," suggested Joshua, "is for me to hike back to the highway and see if I can get a passing car to stop and help us out."

His father agreed that it might be worth trying. So without further delay he set forth. He had gone about a hundred yards when he noticed that the solitary walker, who had been quite forgotten in the face of events, was now getting near. Their paths were going to converge.

Joshua could now see that what, in the distance, had appeared to be a tiny figure lost in a huge landscape was really a very large man who covered ground with long swinging strides. He carried a rifle over one shoulder, and there was some sort of a bag, or pouch, slung on his back. Casually observing the approaching stranger, the boy stopped short in his tracks to get a better look. Could this really be Jedediah Meade, or was his imagination playing a trick?

It *was* Jedediah Meade, and this time he seemed more astonished to see the boy than Joshua was to see him. After their several recent encounters it was beginning to seem as though the old man could almost be counted on to show up in any sort of emergency. They shook hands, grinning at each other broadly and wordlessly. Joshua was the first to find his tongue. He explained that he was headed East with his parents, pointed out the car, and disclosed their predicament. As they stood talking, Mr. and Mrs. Beacon, moved by curiosity, strolled toward them to find out what was going on.

Joshua was glad to be able to introduce old Meade to his mother and father, who, for their part, were obviously somewhat puzzled by this incongruous friendship between their son and a wandering stranger of such extraordinary appearance. But the old man, with characteristic directness, broke the ice by promptly turning his attention to the matter of the flat tire. "This child don't know much about automobiles an' such," he said as he squatted down to peer under the front of the car, "but we can get that thing hoisted up someway, I reckon."

He leaned his rifle carefully against the running board and unslung the bulky leather pouch that hung on his back. Standing loftily beside the low car, he looked as if he might be able to pick up the front end with his great gnarled hands. "About a mile back thataway," he went on, "there's a creek. It's mighty near dry but there's a few trees, an' one of 'em's been split by lightin'. It wouldn't take much of a piece of timber to prize that wheel up off the ground."

Mr. Beacon began to protest politely, but before he had said half a dozen words the old man was striding away in the direction he had indicated. When Joshua called after him to ask if he needed any help he got merely a wave of the arm in reply, which seemed to indicate that he should stay where he was.

An hour or more passed, and it was getting dark when the old man returned. On his shoulder he carried a log about eight or nine feet long and ten inches thick. Getting the car jacked up was then a matter of placing a large stone in position as a fulcrum and laying the log across it with one end firmly under the axle and the other sticking up in front of the car. Old Meade's strength was in direct proportion to his gigantic size, both of which he now applied to the protruding end of the improvised lever. Mr.

Beacon and Joshua aided him with all the power they could muster, and the front left wheel was lifted high enough to permit changing the tire. Joshua then got down on the ground, and while the others held, he stacked several boulders under the axle to keep it up. This done, the flat was easily changed.

The job completed and the tools restored to their proper place, Joshua got into the car to try to drive the front end off the improvised jack. He stepped on the starter but nothing happened. The engine was dead.

His father lifted the hood and together they checked the engine as best they could. But neither was enough of a mechanic to locate the trouble. By now it was dark. Jedediah Meade had disappeared again, but his rifle and shoulder pouch were where he had left them, so he was still somewhere around.

For a few minutes the Beacons hardly knew what to do next. The starter was tried again several times but to no avail. At last it was agreed that their original plan to try to get help from the highway was all that was left to them. So Joshua set out in that direction as he had already once started to do. This time his progress was uninterrupted except by the rocks and ruts that caused him to stumble now and then. A twenty-minute walk brought him to his destination.

He stood a long time beside the road before a car came. As it approached he waved his arms to attract attention, but it whizzed by without so much as slowing down. Again he had a long wait before he saw the distant headlights of an oncoming car. But it too passed without stopping. What few drivers were abroad after dark were evidently unwilling to take a chance of being stopped by a bandit and held up, or worse, on this lonesome road.

Joshua turned away in discouragement. Glancing back in the direction of where he had left his parents, he caught sight of a faint red glow.

What was going on back there? he wondered uneasily. Perhaps he had better go back and investigate. Anyway, there was little use in remaining longer beside the highway if the few cars that did come along were not going to stop. So reasoning, he began to retrace his steps. As he got near to the stalled car he found that the glow he had seen from the road was caused by an open fire burning on the ground.

Jedediah Meade had brought wood and water from the creek and had made Mr. and Mrs. Beacon comfortable beside a cheerful campfire. They were seated on the ground with their backs against a car seat, watching the old man, who was absorbed in cooking something. He looked up from the fire as Joshua approached. "Hullo!" he called out, "I was just goin' to fetch ye. We got some vittles nearly ready."

"What is it?" asked Joshua, bending over and sniffing the meat that was cooking on spits made of green sticks.

"Rabbit," said Jedediah. "I shot two this mornin'."

The two rabbits hardly made a sumptuous meal, but what there was tasted good, and with the addition of some fruit and cookies which were in the car the assembled company was at least spared the discomfort of going supperless.

Warm, comfortable, and fed, it was not difficult for the Beacons to forget, for the time being, the annoying circumstances that had put them in this position. Joshua, as a matter of fact, would not have been willing to trade a suite of rooms in the best hotel in the country for this fireside under the stars, and he had an idea that his parents shared his sentiments to a large degree.

After the meal Jedediah Meade fished into his miraculous pouch and came up with a harmonica on which he played old tunes like "Oh, Susannah" and "On Top of Old Smoky." Pretty soon the others were joining in and singing to his music. When he grew tired of playing he told

stories about fighting Indians and hunting buffalo until, at
last, they were all ready to turn in and get some sleep.

There were two blankets in the car. Mr. and Mrs. Beacon
took one and Joshua the other. The old man said he could
get along fine without any. Joshua rolled up near the fire
in his, made himself as comfortable as the hard ground permitted, and had fallen sound asleep in a matter of minutes.

When he woke up the first glimmer of dawn was lighting the desolate hills. His mother and father were asleep.
Of Meade there was no sign. His rifle and pouch were no
longer in sight. He had gone. Joshua was hardly surprised.
His frontier friend was a man of sudden appearances and
abrupt departures. There was no use worrying about him.
In his own peculiar way he was more than able to take
care of himself.

Joshua got to his feet and stretched. He was stiff from lying on the ground, but he had slept soundly nonetheless. Now his eyes fell on the car and he remembered that its failure to start was the reason they were here. He walked to it, got in, and put his foot on the starter. To his surprise it responded. Last night it had been completely dead. He tried it again and the engine caught, coughed a few times, and then ran.

The sound woke Mr. and Mrs. Beacon. They got up, their stiffness and soreness quickly forgotten as they realized that Joshua had the car going. As they gathered up the blankets, put the seat back in its place, and quickly made ready to depart, the sun came up, modeling the hills with glittering light and crisp blue shadows. Each stone and pebble threw its dark shadow across the bare ground. It was going to be a beautiful day.

With Joshua at the wheel, the Beacons left their camp site and proceeded cautiously to the highway. As he watched the bright day assert itself the boy thought of how pleasant last evening around the fire had been; with a sudden flood of comprehension it dawned on him that the pioneer life in the Western wilds, for all its trials and hardships, must have been glorious. On a day like this, for instance, how good it would be if, instead of stepping into an automobile and pointing it along a paved road, he could be one of an emigrant party hitching their teams and making up the wagon train for a day's march, a day of adventure, a day of living history. . . .

His father's voice broke into his reverie. "What's come over you, Josh? The road is as straight and open as a race track. We've got to make time today. You're poking along at thirty miles an hour."

Joshua sighed and stepped on the gas.